THE TEMPLE
OF DEATH

THE TEMPLE OF DEATH

E.C. TUBB

WILDSIDE PRESS

INTRODUCTION

BY PHILIP HARBOTTLE

In 1954, a young British science fiction writer by the name of E.C. Tubb was on a winning streak of high productivity. Since making his debut in 1951 with a short story "No Short Cuts" in *New Worlds* magazine, he had published more than 50 SF magazine stories and some thirty novels in the space of only four years, and had just turned full-time professional writer. At that time, he was in fact pursuing two literary careers: for the SF magazines, he was writing fascinating stories which explored psychology and human nature. These mature, adult stories won considerable acclaim from his readers, particularly his realistic stories of Martian colonization (eventually collected as *Alien Dust.*) But as a *novelist*, he was obliged to tailor his stories to suit the emerging British market of the "mushroom" publishers who were springing up everywhere, created by post-war austerity and paper rationing.

As he recalled in a memoir: "…the formula they wanted…was to have twelve chapters each of three thousand words, each chapter, if possible, ending on a high point. It was a mechanical technique and led to stories that were more a series of episodes rather than a closely plotted story. But I enjoyed writing them and found the concentration on action easier to handle than the interplay of deep characterization, a style both difficult to do within the confines of the length and unwanted by the publishers. Fast-moving adventure stories against colourful backgrounds—a formula which is still the best for easily-assimilated entertainment. I could write this kind of fiction and had no trouble selling…"

Tubb was adept at adapting the exciting ideas and themes of the early pulp SF magazines with his own special brand of realism and logic. As noted above, the bibliographical record credits Tubb with thirty novels—*but he had in fact written thirty-two.*

The boom in British SF pocket books issued by these mushroom publishers came to an abrupt end in 1954. The complex reasons for this blight that settled on British science fiction have been identified and analysed in my book, *Vultures of the Void: The Legacy* (2012), and more recently discussed on my "1950s British Science Fiction Paperbacks" YouTube videos, and so do not need to be gone into here. Suffice it to say that Tubb's last two adventure novels, *The Spore Menace* and *The Temple of Vra-Vheera*, written back-to-back in the summer of 1954, fell back into his hands.

But whilst by 1954 the British market for adventure science fiction was dying, *in European countries it was just beginning*, spearheaded by the French publisher Fleuve Noir. In their *Anticipation* series of novels, which began by featuring such French writers as Jimmy Gieu and F.R. Bessiere, they began to introduce an increasing number of translations of John Russell Fearn's "Vargo Statten" novels. They were immediately successful, and paved the way for other English writers—including E.C. Tubb. The French translations were in turn translated into Italian, Danish, Portugese, and German. Thus encouraged, Tubb dug out his two old unsold novels and passed the original mss. to

Anna Steul, a young German fan and literary agent, whom he had he had met at a British SF Convention. She promised to try and make a sale to the still-burgeoning German market, where Tubb was becoming well known in translation. *The Spore Menace* was subsequently sold to a German publisher in 1960, but the second novel appeared to have been lost.

Meanwhile, with a new mortgage and a young family to support, Tubb sought new directions. He diversified into other literary genres—westerns, detective, foreign legion, and war-fiction comic strips—and by concentrating on his quality SF magazine short stories, he cracked the much more lucrative American market.

But with no immediate UK market in sight, the author put the carbon copies of his two unsold novels away in a drawer and forgot about them. They remained unpublished in English for more than 40 years, until I became Tubb's agent, and on learning of their existence I had them retyped, after which they quickly sold to a U.S. small press under the new titles of *Pandora's Box* and *Temple of Death*.

Superficially, *The Temple of Death* is dated. Most of the action takes place on Mars—a Mars with a breathable atmosphere and inhabited by a race of humanoid Martians. This was a common background to early SF adventure fiction, but in the light of astronomical discoveries many would consider it unpublishable today. Unpublishable? Not necessarily!

In the hands of a master story teller—most famously Edgar Rice Burroughs—a habitable Mars is just another literary framing device. A powerful story can transcend its background, and the early Martian stories can today be enjoyed as science fantasy.

Tubb's basic ideas employed in this novel remain fascinating today: the Martians have a secret religion, the cult of the Dra Vheera, which is forbidden to Earthmen. A picked band of mercenaries—victims of the taboo, and with good reason to hate Martians—are hired to go on a secret mission to Mars. Their objective is to penetrate the secrets of a Martian temple and rip aside the veil of secrecy. The unravelling of the mystery is vintage Tubb, involving human and alien psychology, interpreted through the medium of high adventure and explosive, pulse-pounding action.

The intriguing theme has echoes of a much older story, written by Clifford D. Simak—"The Voice in the Void," published in the Spring 1932 *Wonder Stories Quarterly*. Simak's story tells of the desecration of a sacred Martian tomb, where Earthmen make the astounding discovery that the sacred bones of the Martian Messiah are those of an Earthman! Tubb's denouement is quite different, but no less astounding. It is certainly possible that Tubb had once read Simak's story, since he was a voracious reader of the American pulp magazines in his youth, when remaindered copies of American pulp magazines were imported into Britain.

But enough preamble. The stage has been set. This new Wildside edition, part of a special series rediscovering E.C. Tubb's SF novels, is your own personal time machine. So settle back and enjoy this rousing 1950s adventure classic!

CHAPTER ONE

DESPERATE THEFT

Night came like a tired old woman spreading her tattered cloak over the fading remains of the dying day. Stars blossomed fitfully in the darkening bowl of the sky, then, touched by the ebon fingers of unlit clouds, blinked and vanished in wispy memory. A wind arose, a thin, sighing, keening wind, droning from the frozen plains of the north and carrying on its invisible wings chill and moisture, bitterness and the threat of early winter. Shadows thickened and lights flared like trapped fireflies in the canyons of the streets, fighting with the mechanical efficiency of science, the age-old laws of nature.

Rain came, thin and penetrating, filtering down from the star-shielding clouds, flurried by the chill wind, washing streets and buildings, trickling in the gutters and filling the sewers on its inevitable way to the distant sea. It fell on glassite-covered penthouses, on the broad acres of concrete which was the landing field, the wide roads and the twisting lanes. It fell on people, on the surging crowds spilling from office and shop, from mono-rail and moving way. It wetted them all, the well-fed and the hungry, the satisfied and the discontent, the hopeful and those to whom hope was an aching memory.

It fell on Colin.

He stood on the edge of the sidewalk, a tall man, his cropped head bare and the rash of blue pockmarks on one cheek dulled by the stubble of a three-day beard. His eyes were grey, the cold, hard grey of freshly quarried slate, his chin was firm and his mouth was a twisted line of bitterness and hate. Around him people moved in swift impatience to escape the rain, brightly dressed men and women, some in their work blouses of shimmering cellosilk, others in their relaxation clothes of multi-coloured materials. Among them, dressed as he was in faded blouse and trousers, short leather jacket and high knee-boots, he was as conspicuous as a piece of coal among diamonds, as a swallow among gaudy plumaged birds of paradise.

Too conspicuous.

A patrol car swung around a corner and slowed with a falling whine from its turbine engine. It slid to a halt and uniformed men sprang from the vehicle, moving with practiced efficiency as they closed in on the solitary figure. Colin stared at them, not moving, not lifting his hands from where they rested, thumbs tucked behind the belt he wore around his waist.

"Your iden." One of the patrolmen thrust out his hand while his companion stood a yard further back, his hand resting on the stungun at his belt.

"This what you mean?" Colin fumbled in a pocket and produced a slip of heat-treated plastic.

"That's it." The patrolman snatched it and stared at it with expert eyes. It bore a photograph, double thumbprints, retinal pattern, code number, and a succession of punched holes and symbols. It told all that needed to be known about the owner, all he had done, could do, where he had been, how long he had stayed, everything. In itself it was a perfect, unforgeable document combining all the attributes of passport, birth certificate, employment records and health chart.

"Seems correct." The patrolman's eyes flickered from the features before him to the sealed photograph. "From Mars, eh?"

"That's right."

"What are you doing in town?"

"That's my business." Colin stared at the uniformed man. "Is there a law against my standing here?"

"There might be. Loitering with intent to steal, for example." The guard flipped the plastic identity card against his thumbnail. "Better not get too smart, fellow. We can do without your sort here."

"My sort?" The big man didn't alter the tone of his voice but something burned with brief fire deep within the cold grey eyes. The patrolman shrugged.

"Nothing personal, you understand, but you people aren't popular now. They kicked you off Mars for a reason and that's good enough for us." He flicked the identity card again. "Take my advice and stay out of the business section, at least until you can get washed up and wear some decent clothes. We've got our job to do and we're going to do it. Get moving now."

"A job!" Colin stared contemptuously at the uniformed man. "What sort of a job do you call that? Shoving people around who haven't the strength to shove back?" He sneered. "I've met men like you before, lackeys, boot-lickers, yellow cowards without that gun at your belt. To hell with you!"

"That's enough!" The patrolman stepped forward, all friendliness forgotten in the face of the big man's undisguised contempt, and the little slip of plastic made a slapping sound as he threw it against the faded leather jacket. He didn't watch it fall to the dirty street. "You heard what I said. Move, and keep moving. If we spot you again, we'll run you in."

"For what? Breathing?" Colin took a deep breath. "Look, sonny. They threw me off Mars and there wasn't a man up there with guts enough to stand up for me. I had to stand being pushed around because there wasn't anything else I could do. Down here it's different. Down here I've got nothing to lose. Now get the hell away from me before I lose my temper."

"I've warned you, Colin." The patrolman made a gesture towards his companion and the stungun the other had drawn slipped back into its holster. "Remember this, you! If we spot you again around here, you're in trouble. Mars scum aren't wanted here and don't you forget it!" He stared at the big man, his hand resting on his holster as though he would welcome an opportunity to use the stungun and freeze Colin into twitching paralysis, then, scowling, turned towards the waiting patrol car. Doors slammed and the turbine hum rose to a shrilling whine as the vehicle slid away.

For a long time Colin stared after it, oblivious to the curious stares of hurrying pedestrians as they looked wonderingly as the solitary, shabby figure standing in the rain. He was sweating, great oozing drops mingling with the rain, and his hands trembled a little as he looked down at them. He swallowed, took a deep of breath and, slowly, stooped and picked up the identity card.

He tucked it back into a pocket as he walked away.

A turnstile admitted him to a moving way, the automatic locking device taking all but a few of his last coins, and he followed the fluorescent signs as he walked down towards the conveyor belts. It was a local station, only three belts with a maximum speed of fifteen miles an hour, and he jumped on the strip heading north, stepping easily from the slow, to the intermediate, and then to the fast belt with half-conscious coordination of his muscles.

A man approached him as he settled himself on the central leaning strip.

"Hi, mister! Stranger here?"

Colin stared at him, noting the shifty eyes, the furtive expression, the pasty white features and the flashy though obviously inexpensive garments. He shrugged, not answering, the moving ways were infested with touts and petty criminals, beggars and con-men, peddlers and those living on the fringe of respectable society.

"Just in from the field?" The stranger grinned and Colin guessed that he had been mistaken for a newly arrived spacemen. He stared thoughtfully at the little man.

"That's right."

"Looking for a time?" The stranger leaned forward and the butt of a weapon showed momentarily beneath his jacket. "I know just the place for a man who's been too long in space." He winked. "You know what I mean?"

"Sensatapes?"

"That's right." The tout stared over his shoulder. "The real thing too, not the watered-down stuff you get in the legit theatres. See, feel, taste, hear, the whole works." He winked again. "Interested?"

"I might be." Colin fingered the few coins in his pocket. "How much?"

"A hundred—or maybe less to a friend."

"How much less?"

"Seventy-five." The tout licked his lips. "You got it?"

"Sure," lied Colin and edged a little nearer to the man. "More than that if it's necessary. You want it now?" He slipped one hand into a pocket as if to take out money, his grey eyes never flickering from the pasty features of the little tout.

"Loaded, eh?" The stranger licked his lips and stared over his shoulder. His arm lifted a little, the material of his cheap blouse tightening over his upper arm and when he turned, it was with deceptive speed. Colin grunted as he reached forward and gripped a thin wrist.

"Impatient, friend?" He smiled without humour as he twisted, his strong fingers grinding against bone and the tout whimpered as he felt his fingers grow numb. "Trying to rob me? Shoot me down because you thought I had money?"

"No!" Sweat shone on the pasty features and the lips writhed back to reveal rotting teeth. "I was just…"

He grunted, a soft exhalation no louder than the driving impact of the fist against his jaw, then sagged against the central leaning strip. Colin glanced around him, still supporting the unconscious man, then, slipping the gun from the concealed holster into his own pocket, propped the would-be thief against the plastic and stepped quickly towards slow belt and the approaching facade of a station.

The weapon wasn't much, a needler, capable of firing an anaesthetic dart through normal clothing at ten feet and rendering a man unconscious within two seconds. Unconscious or dead, depending on whether the tiny darts were poisoned or relatively harmless. A short-range weapon, typical of those used in the cities, a thief's weapon, an assassin's, a tool to be used where the snarl of a high velocity gun, the whine of a stungun or the roaring thunder of an energy weapon would be something to be avoided. A nasty weapon.

Colin examined it in the light of an overhead beacon, turning it over in his palm and checking the load. It was good to be armed again. The feel of the smooth metal gave a sense of power, a touch of the old life when a gun was a normal part of his everyday wear and a man carried his own law at his waist. He sighed, remembering the patrol and the way they had examined him. To be found with an unlicensed weapon, especially such a weapon as this, would be to invite ten years hard labour on the Hell Planet. He didn't want to be sent to Mercury. Neither did he want to throw the gun away, for guns cost money, and he had no money, and unless he obtained some soon…

He slipped the weapon into his pocket, and walked towards the poorer section of the city.

The place he was looking for wasn't hard to find. It rested on a corner, fitting into its environment as if it had grown there, which it probably had and around it hung an undefinable odour of must and decay, of dust and cobwebs. An impression, of course, for in this day and age cobwebs and dust were a thing of the past in the big cities, or should have been. Other impressions weren't so intangible. The wide, brilliantly lit windows were filled with fragments and debris from a thousand homes, a curiously carved piece of stone from the humid jungles of Venus, a broken short-range transceiver, a glittering heap of baubles, some odd items of clothing, the accumulated junk of those who had tried too hard and failed. He stared at them, fingering the pistol in his pocket, knowing that this of all places would be the one most likely to buy and, above his head, swinging a little in the bitter wind, the age-old sign of those who lent money against goods cast sprawling shadows over the rain-washed street.

The pawnbroker seemed to have grown with his shop. A fat man, wheezing a little as he waddled from a back room, the soft flesh of his throat sagging over the frayed collar of his blouse and his little, fat-wreathed eyes, shrewd and calculating as he stared at the big man.

"Yes?"

Colin kicked shut the door behind him and his long legs carried him in three strides to the low counter. "You buy things?"

"Of course, and lend money against them if you so desire." The fat man shrugged. "You have something to sell?"

"Yes." Colin slipped the pistol from his pocket and laid it on the counter. "This."

"A gun!" The pawnbroker glanced sharply at his customer. "Licensed, of course?"

"No."

"No?" The fat man shrugged, his tremendous shoulders shifting beneath his blouse in the typical gesture of his kind. "Then…"

"Look," snapped Colin urgently. "All I want is to sell it, how I got it doesn't concern you and you needn't worry about a come-back. I'll forget everything as soon as I leave here."

"Not so fast, my friend." The fat man picked up the weapon and examined it with expert eyes. "A needler, loaded too, and one of the late models." His little eyes narrowed. "Poison?"

"I don't know."

"Indeed? Isn't this weapon yours?"

"I want to sell it," said the big man curtly. "If you are willing to buy, then we can do business, if not I'll try somewhere else." He held out his hand. "Give me the gun."

"A moment." The pawnbroker made no attempt to hand over the weapon. "Do you know the penalty for carrying in an unlicensed weapon?"

"Perhaps."

"Ten years on Mercury without parole, and no excuses are acceptable." He jiggled the weapon on the palm of his plump hand. "The same penalty applies to anyone who sells or purchases such a weapon. This is dangerous merchandise you bring me, my friend. Too dangerous."

"Then forget it." Colin reached over and with a smoothly coordinated movement took the gun from the pawnbroker's hand. "If you don't want to buy it, that's good enough. I'll try elsewhere."

"Wait!" The fat man smiled as Colin turned, halfway towards the door. "I must warn you that you have been photographed and recorded. Also, the door is locked and you are covered with a stungun. I take no chances, my friend— you will stay as you are." He smiled again as the big man levelled the weapon. "Try it if you wish, but shouldn't you have these?" He opened his left hand and displayed the small charge-clip for the weapon. "I unloaded it," he explained. "I have not kept a shop all these years without learning to take a few elementary precautions."

"What's the idea?" Colin squeezed the trigger of the needler as he spoke and knew from the dry click that the fat man spoke the truth. He reversed the weapon, balancing it in his hand, and drew his arm back for the throw, then, just as he was about to hurl the useless gun into the smiling fat features, he doubled in an ecstasy of pain.

Liquid fire traced every nerve and probed every cell. His muscles knotted and a great, invisible hand, seemed to be squeezing his heart. Blackness surged around him, a thundering tide of incipient oblivion, and dimly he heard the metallic thud as the weapon fell from his numbed hand.

"That's better." The pain lifted a little and Colin stared through pain-filled eyes at the bland features of the fat man. "I warned you that you were covered by a stungun, and, at low charge, a stungun can be most painful."

"What are you going to do?" Blood filled the big man's mouth as he tried to control the burning paralysis of his tortured body.

"Do?" The pawnbroker seemed amused. "Turn you over to the patrol, of course, what else should I do?"

"You could let me go. I've done you no harm."

"Perhaps not, but you could do me some good. After all, there is a reward for any citizen turning in a criminal, and any man who carries an unlicensed weapon is automatically a criminal." The fat man shrugged. "Sorry, my friend, but you see how it is. You are worth a hundred credits to me and a man must eat."

"Yes." Sweat stung the big man's blood-shot eyes as he tried to edge nearer to the smiling man. "A man must eat. Damn you! I've met your sort on Mars, smug, smiling, yellow-bellied rats who only think of their own stomachs. To hell with you!"

"Mars?" Abruptly the nerve-gripping energy of the hidden stungun faded a little and Colin straightened himself with a grunt of relief. "You have been on Mars?"

"Yes."

"How long ago? When did you return?"

"I came back on Earth four weeks ago. Why?"

"Why?" The pawnbroker shrugged. "Perhaps nothing. Perhaps everything." He nodded. "Yes, I think…"

"You think what?"

"Sorry, my friend, I would have like to avoid this, but…" Again he shrugged, the faded material of his frayed blouse writhing over his obese body, and one hand fell below the top of the low counter.

Colin guessed what was about to happen and, guessing, tried to escape. Muscles throbbed in protest as he flung himself forward, his hands hooked and reaching towards the loose flesh of the sagging throat. One step he took, two, then with savage abruptness, energy lashed at him, the numb, nerve-shocking energy of a stungun at full aperture, and consciousness and reason vanished before the pulse of that irresistible force.

He didn't feel the impact as he struck the floor.

CHAPTER TWO

THE DRA VHEERA

Awareness returned like a shy bride, slowly, reluctantly, filtering back with throbbing anguish and searing pain. He groaned, opened his eyes, and carefully sat upright, his hands supporting his head as he sat on something soft and warm.

After a long time he lifted his head and stared around him.

It wasn't a cell. That he could tell after the first glance, for there was no bare concrete, no bars, no harsh utilitarianism about the room in which he sat. A soft carpet covered the floor and smooth, softly lit plastic the walls. A table stood in one corner, and bottles littering its surface, and a desk, a massive thing of polished wood, faced it across the room. Chairs there were, soft and deep, and a few small pictographs hung by their magnetic attachments to the plastic. A normal room, a study perhaps, a room to receive business men or to discuss business. But not a cell, certainly not that.

Slowly he rose, letting life resume its interrupted prerogative, and half-stumbled, half-fell towards the table, his hands and eyes busy examining the bottles. Whisky there was, the genuine product of Scotland. Brandy from the warm vineyards of France. Vodka from the bleak Steppes and Chianti from the sunny slopes of fair Italy. Theondite, that black, bitter, alien brew from the swollen fungi of Venus, and the thin, poisonous green wine of the Hotlands. Zecohl was there, the potent spirit from Mars, distilled from the fermented bodies of sand-lice, and one bottle held the sapphire condensation of Mercurian lichens, the incredibly expensive liquor which few men could drink and remain sane.

He reached for the Zecohl, tilting the fused-sand bottle and letting the familiar spirit gush down his constricted throat. It warmed him, driving the frozen chill of paralysis from his nerves and stomach and, setting down the bottle, he reached for a cigarette and puffed it into glowing life. He killed half the little white cylinder before taking a second drink, letting the liquid rill around his mouth before swallowing and by the time he had smoked the cigarette, he felt almost normal again.

From the stubble on his chin, he guessed that he had been unconscious for almost a day, a long time to be paralysed, and his stomach burned from the potent spirit and lack of food. Impatiently he strode about the room, glaring at the knobless door and knowing that it was a waste of time to try and force the electronic lock. The desk was similarly locked, the walls seamless, the floor solid. Shrugging he returned to the table and, picking up the bottle of Zecohl, sat down on the floor, his back to a wall, and took small sips of the well-remembered liquor, chain-smoking, and letting his tired mind and body rest.

The spirit could have been drugged, or the cigarettes, or perhaps it was the natural response of his overstrained body to the stungun paralysis, but before he had sat there long his eyes closed and he slept.

When he awoke he was no longer alone.

A man sat behind the desk, a small, white-haired, ravaged-featured man, impeccably dressed and with rare stones flashing like trapped and alien eyes from the wide bands of metal circling his fingers. He puffed deliberately at an expensive cigar of imported Venusian tobacco, and the subtle aroma of the exotic weed filled the room with heady fragrance. Colin stared at him, then, rising, stepped towards the desk.

"Who are you?"

Smoke billowed towards him from the cigar and sunken eyes of midnight black stared at him through the writhing clouds. A voice, rustling and dry, almost whispering and yet with a peculiar resonance spilled from between thin, bloodless lips.

"You come from Mars?"

"Yes."

"How long were you on Mars?"

"That's my business." Colin glared at the man. "Who are you? What's all this about?"

"Have patience—you will learn." A thin finger pressed a button and a chair rose silently from the carpeted floor. "Be seated. We have much to discuss."

"Have we?" The big man flexed his hands. "I think not."

"No?" Almost there was humour in the rustling tones, almost, but not quite. Again the paper-thin hands moved and now two objects rested on the polished surface of the huge desk. One of them was familiar, the smooth, neatly fashioned needler, the other…

Colin stared at it, trying to estimate just how many bills rested in the little pile.

"There are a thousand credits there," whispered the dry voice. "They are yours—if you will listen without interruption and answer all my questions."

"And if I don't?"

"You can still be arrested for carrying an unlicensed weapon." The thin fingers caressed the smooth metal. "Well? Which is it to be?"

"I'll listen." Colin slumped into the chair and rasped his fingers over the stubble on his lips and chin. "But first, how did I get here? Who are you?"

"I shall answer those questions in a few moments, but they can wait." The thin man leaned forward. "How long were you on Mars?"

"Ten years."

"So long? That is well. Why did you leave?"

"I was kicked off-planet," said Colin deliberately. "They didn't want me on their damn dust bowl and so they threw me out." Anger drew his mouth into a bitter line. "Ten years I sweated there. Ten years of back-breaking hell and for what? For a one-way ticket back to Earth and the sneers of the fools who call themselves men." He caught himself as the anger rose within him, biting his lips and staring at his trembling hands, reliving again the frustration and hate which had lived with him for too long.

"I was an atomic engineer," he said quietly, and the pockmarked skin on his cheek writhed in ancient memory. "I saved a little money and stopped off at Mars. I behaved myself and built up a nice business, repair and overhaul, new piles and replacement units for the farmers and factories. A nice business. Ten more years and I'd have been able to retire a rich man. Five more years and I'd have put all worry behind me. I didn't get those five years."

"They kicked you out," whispered the thin man. "Why?"

"I forgot, or grew careless, or took too much for granted. Does it matter?"

"Yes. It could matter a lot. Why?"

"The usual thing. I grew a little too curious, but that wasn't it. It was a mistake, a thing which could happen to anyone, but they don't believe in mistakes."

"The Dra Vheera?"

"You know?" Colin stared at the thin man, then shrugged. "You're right, of course, it could only have been the Dra Vheera." He knotted his hands again and his grey eyes clouded as they stared into the past. "I suppose that it had to happen, I'm not the first man to be kicked out, and I doubt if I'll be the last. The Dra Vheera, the priesthood of Mars, the temple, the religion. One name for all three, but all three really one." He stared at the smoke-wreathed figure behind the desk. "But it wasn't fair! I made a mistake, a thing unavoidable, and they crucified me for it!"

"Perhaps."

"You don't believe me, do you? You've heard it all before, the whining complaints, the excuses; the protestations of innocence. Well, to hell with you! I know that I speak the truth."

"I believe you," said the man quietly. "Continue."

"You know how it is," said the big man dully. "We are only tolerated on Mars, the natives don't want us and they make no attempt to disguise their contempt for all Terrestrials. Perhaps they are right, Earthmen have little pride and no culture compared to them, and what little we have is forgotten when we set our foot on the road to exploitation. We need the Martians though, we need the things they produce, the rare, exquisitely beautiful artwork, the hypnotic cadences of their music, and above all we need the Elixir. We are grateful for the Elixir, too grateful, for in our longing for extended life we forget our pride. So Earthmen on Mars are only a tolerated nuisance and we have to tread softly in order to remain."

"I know that," whispered the thin man. "All Earth knows that."

"Yes, and so you can imagine the naked hate directed against anyone who endangers our foothold on the Red Planet. A complaint from the Dra Vheera and a man is ostracised, penalised, treated worse than a criminal. His own friends will turn on him, his own race disown him, and even his own planet regards him as a dangerous criminal. And all this because a Martian priest has informed the Terran Consul that they do not want that man on Mars. A little thing can do it, a look, an expression, a glance. Then a few whispered words, a veiled threat, and…." His hand made a chopping motion. "Finish!"

"The Dra Vheera, of course?"

"Yes. All Earthmen on Mars carry one inflexible, unalterable, inexcusable warning. Never on any account to interfere with, show curiosity about, or attempt to understand the native religion. Never. To even ask a harmless question is equal to banishment, to attempt to photograph a priest, a temple, or even to sketch one, is equal to death." He nodded at the thin man. "Yes. Death as conducted by the Dra Vheera, and there isn't a Terrestrial on Mars who dares oppose them. If they did, then the supplies of Elixir would cease, old men would lose their chance of restored youth, and all our investments on the Red Planet would be lost. So what chance has one man against that? Of what consideration is the life of an individual against all that Mars has to offer? The Dra Vheera rules Mars and everything on it."

"And you?"

"There was a storm," said Colin bitterly. "I was out seeing to a new replacement unit for a broken-down sand car. I'd done the job and was on my way back to the settlement when the storm blew up and within minutes I was blinded by sand and dust. Naturally I lost my way, not much, but I veered from the straight line by a few miles. The next day the Dra Vheera complained that I'd entered the forbidden zone around the temple."

"Did you?"

"I don't know. I may have done so, the storm was pretty bad and it's just possible that I did cut a tangent through the forbidden circle. I didn't know it, the storm was too bad for me to even see more than a few yards ahead, and certainly I didn't see the temple, but they wouldn't accept excuses. I'd entered the forbidden zone, it may have only been a few hundred feet, but it was enough. I was finished."

"As simple as that?" The thin man nodded, seeming almost pleased by the big man's bitterness.

"Yes. They stripped me of everything I owned, fined me, sent me back on the very next rocket, a pauper, and dumped me on a planet which I'd almost forgotten. Ten year's work thrown away. All my possessions seized and all my money taken as fines for breaking the Dra Vheera code of conduct. They couldn't have treated me worse had I murdered a dozen Terrestrials. And even on Earth I'm treated as something worse than a murderer."

Silence fell then, a silence broken only by the small sounds made by the thin man as he sucked at his cigar and the harsh rasping of breath in the big man's throat. It lasted for perhaps a whole minute, then the thin man sighed and carefully rested his cigar on the edge of an ashtray.

"Do you hate Mars?"

"You ask me that?" Colin thinned his lips as he let some of his bitterness seep into his tones. "After what they did to me? I hate Mars and everything about it. I hate the fat and slimy Earthmen who are only too willing to throw one of their number to the dogs in order to be allowed to make money. I hate the Martians for their arrogance and undisguised contempt. I hate the natives but I hate the Terrestrials more for they have forgotten their pride and the Martians are only as strong as they are allowed to be." He took a sobbing breath. "If I could only..."

"Hurt them?" The thin man nodded. "I understand." He hesitated, his black eyes thoughtful as he looked at Colin. "First, let me explain that I have been looking for men like you. The pawnbroker knew that and, when he learned you were from Mars, took my offer of a double reward to deliver you to me instead of to the patrolmen." He gestured with one ringed hand. "So much for that. As for the rest..." He pushed the little heap of money across the desk. "This is yours—if you will help me."

"Help you?" Colin stared blankly at the man. "How?"

"My name," said the thin man deliberately, "is Barnhart." He smiled at the big man's expression of recognition. "You know of me?"

"A little. Rich, incredibly rich, the first man to engage in the Elixir trade with Mars. You have a son..."

"I had a son." Pain filled the old man's voice as he made the correction. "A boy who, to me, was worth all the System put together. I would have done anything for him, did everything I could, but he was a Barnhart and insisted on going his own way." He paused. "He went to Mars."

"I think that I remember now," said Colin slowly. "It must be a few years ago now, there was some scandal, some unpleasantness…?"

"My son was found mutilated and dead shortly after his arrival." Barnhart bit off the words as though he found their taste unpleasant as he probably did. "My son was interested in comparative religions and had gone to Mars to study the Dra Vheera."

"Then he was a fool," said Colin curtly. "He should have known better."

"As you should have done?" The thin man shrugged. "Recriminations are a waste of time. My son died, died in a horrible manner, his body mutilated almost beyond recognition, his head missing."

"Missing?" Colin blinked. "You mean that he'd been decapitated?"

"Yes."

"I see." The big man stared thoughtfully at his hands then shrugged. "So he's dead. So what?"

"So I want to avenge him." Barnhart leaned forward across his desk and light flashed from his fingers as the soft illumination reflected from the rings he wore. "He was my only son, Colin," he said, and almost it seemed as if his voice would break. "My only son, and by all the Gods of space someone's going to pay for his death!"

"Then all Mars should pay, for the Dra Vheera is Mars."

"Exactly." Barnhart sighed as he relaxed in the chair. "What do you know of their religion, Colin?"

"Nothing, the same as any other Terrestrial."

"And yet, after ten years on Mars, you must have gained some knowledge. What can you remember, guess, surmise? What is so special about the Temple of Dra Vheera?"

"If I knew the answers to those questions, I wouldn't be alive now," said the big man grimly. "They are the things your son tried to discover, and you know what happened him. No Earthman has ever been inside the temple. No Terrestrial has any real knowledge of the Martian religion at all."

"But you can guess?"

"Yes," admitted Colin slowly. "I can guess." He stared at the thin man. "I lived ten years on Mars and all that time the Dra Vheera was a perpetual challenge. A mystery, and I don't like mysteries. A problem which I wanted to solve, and yet dared not. An ominous brooding thing affecting the lives of everything on the planet." He paused and when he spoke again, his voice was the voice of a man who speaks from the past.

"It is more than a religion; the Dra Vheera is an actual way of life. The priests literally have the power of life and death and they rule the entire planet. And yet they do it without the use of force, even with the Earthmen they use no force. Threats are enough. Your son died, but he wasn't the only one. More than one body has been found in the desert, stripped and tormented, decapitated and violated. Fools who refused to take the warnings seriously, men who tried to see too much and who paid for their temerity with their lives. Paid horribly in a manner we can only guess. They are the ones who tried to get into the temple, or who questioned a little too closely, who refused to be warned, who struck their necks out too far.

"But some things I do know, or at least can make a guess at. There is something in the temple which every Martian reveres more than life itself, something which forms the focal point of their religion." He glanced at the intent features of the old man. "You want revenge? Then why not drop a bomb on the temple?"

"And if I did? What then?"

"A blood-bath. The natives would kill every Terrestrial on Mars. But you couldn't do that, of course, the Patrol would blast you out of space as soon as you entered the forbidden zone." He hesitated. "Anyway, I doubt if a normal bomb, even an atomic one, could do much harm to the temple."

"What makes you say that?" Barnhart's eyes glittered in the soft lighting as he stared at the big man.

"I don't really know, just an impression I have, an inner conviction. Mars is pretty old, millions of years older than Earth, and the natives seem to have aged with the planet. There are little things, their awareness of events which they should have known nothing about, a kind of precognition if you like. My own case proves it. No one could possibly have seen me in that storm, and yet the Dra Vheera knew that I had entered the zone. How?" He shrugged. "Not that it matters. Their bare word was enough to blacklist me and get me thrown off-planet."

"So you told me." Barnhart examined his fingernails and then reached for his still-smouldering cigar. "But you miss the point. I have no intention of dropping a bomb on their temple, for that would be foolish. No. I want to avenge my son, I want to hurt every Martian as they have hurt me. I want them to remember what they did and regret it." He paused and writhing clouds of smoke made a drifting veil before his glittering black eyes. "I want to do the very thing they would give their souls to avoid."

"I begin to see what you mean," said Colin quietly. "But how?"

"They worship whatever is in that temple. They guard their religion with a fanatical determination. The Dra Vheera rules Mars and yet the Dra Vheera is a mystery. My son vanished to solve that mystery. He died because of it. I want to do what he failed to do."

"Ridicule." Colin nodded and something feral and not quite human shone in the depths of his grey eyes. "Find out what it is all about. Violate their most sacred beliefs and broadcast what the Dra Vheera is to the ends of the System. Tear away their mystery, send them crazy with hate and fear and frustration." He licked his lips and looked at the thin figure behind the desk. "A dream, but an impossible one. Earth would never allow it. They would use the Patrol Fleet to hunt you down even if you merely tried it. They would defend the Dra Vheera with every weapon in their arsenals."

"Yes."

"To attempt to do as you wish is hopeless." He shrugged. "Oh, I've thought about it. Every man on Mars must have done it one time or another. To get into the temple, to watch their rites, to get out alive, and stay alive…" He shook his head. "Some have tried it, your son among them, and you know what happened to him."

"Yes."

"It's impossible! And yet?" He smiled with a terrible lack of humour. "To rip away the veil they have tried so hard to keep. To watch them squirm, all of them, natives and Terrestrials alike, and to sit back and laugh, and laugh, and keep on laughing! Gods of Space! What a revenge that would be!"

"Yes."

"You know what it would mean, of course? Mars would turn into a shambles and all trading would stop. Earthmen would be at literal war with the natives—a war which they may not win. Is it worth it?"

"My son died," said Barnhart quietly. "I want to avenge his death and what better way than by doing the very thing for which he was murdered?"

"Yes," said Colin. "I know how you feel."

"I intend to violate the temple of Dra Vheera on Mars and publish the results of what is found." Fragrant smoke belied the hidden inference of the calm words. "I am intelligent enough to evaluate the risks but I accept them. Will you?"

"I don't know." Colin stared down at his hands and within him twin emotions warred for dominance. On the one side burning hate and a desire for revenge on the society which had cost him all he possessed. On the other the intelligent realisation that the Martians had a right to their own way of life on their own planet.

"Ten years," whispered the old man. "Ten years of heartbreak and hope, gone in a flash through no fault of your own. Now you are an outcast, unwanted on either world, a pauper driven to risk the Hell Planet and with nothing but sneers and starvation, charity or menial labour to look forward to. They did that to you, the same people who murdered my son. Are you so weak that you will allow them to drive you away from what is yours and do nothing about it?"

The whispering voice swung the balance. The awakened memories of what he had lost blinded him to logic and cold calculation. Anger swept him and the burning what he had been ate into his indecision. Colin stared at man behind the desk.

"I'm with you," he gritted. "What do you want me to do?"

Barnhart smiled and within their sunken pits of his ebon eyes glittered like the smouldering coals of hell.

CHAPTER THREE

MARTIAN LANDING

The ship was a wallowing nightmare, a hastily patched collection of junk, more fit for the scrapyard than for venturing into the void. The plates leaked, the escaping air bringing a frigid chill to the cramped interior, and the obsolete rocket engines threatened to rip themselves free of their mountings every time they were fired. Rust and mildew clung to the bulkheads, half the instruments were broken, and those which still operated were erratic and unreliable. The ship would never have been rewarded a space-worthiness certificate, no decent crew would have considered signing on, and no merchant, no matter how desperate, would have trusted cargo to its rotting holds.

But, despite that, the ship had crew and cargo, passengers and destination.

Colin walked through the vessel, checking the quarters, the cargo, glancing at the passengers as they lounged in their bunks or sat around a table playing with magnetic-backed cards. A rough, hard-bitten, hard-handed collection of men. Most of them had come from the gutters of the big cities, some were wanted by the law; others had sold themselves for gain as had the mercenaries of old. All of them had, at one time or another, been kicked off Mars.

He had recruited them, combing the doss houses and charity wards, haunting the slums and watching the labour bureau. One by one he had found them, tested them, told them all he thought they should know, fed their hate and offered high reward, and now they formed one of the strangest private armies ever to have taken the field. Looking at them, Colin knew that he had chosen well.

Captain Manson looked up from his instruments as the big man entered the control room.

"Hello, Colin. How are the passengers behaving?"

"Well enough." Colin stared at the ranked instruments and at the star-shot blackness of space beyond the direct vision ports. Earth lay somewhere behind them, a dim green point almost lost among the glittering stars, the Moon had dwindled and lost itself in distance, and now the ship was on the last lap on its long journey, coasting in free fall towards the glowing ball that was Mars.

"How's the ship?"

"Rotten!" Manson turned from his instruments and stared disgustedly at the dirt and mildew marring the once-bright metal of bulkheads and floorplates. "I've put Free-guard in the engine room, if anyone can get those motors to behave he can. Wilner is checking the air conditioners and I'm trying to plot a course with equipment at least ten percent unreliable. This tub is a wreck, Colin, it's a mystery to me why we didn't rip ourselves apart during take-off."

"It was cheap and it will do the job." Colin sat in one of the worn acceleration chairs and stared at the grizzled captain. Like all the men aboard the vessel Manson had good cause to hate Mars. A spaceship captain, he had commanded one of the crack express liners until an electronic storm had thrown his vessel off-course and into the ten thousand mile wide forbidden area applicable to all spaceships. There had been no enquiry, no excuses, the Dra Vheera had complained and Manson had been stripped of his command, returned to Earth, and there left to rot his life away in a cheap hotel.

The others were the same. Freeguard, an engineer, a wizard with rocket engines, a man who had drunk a little too much Zecohl and had insulted a Martian priest. Wilner, a man who had stared too long at the temple and who had paid for his curiosity with all he possessed. Barker, a big, silent man. He'd once had a wife until the Dra Vheera had accused him of wandering too often near the ten mile forbidden zone around the temple. His wife had divorced him then, and he had been kicked off-planet. There were others, many others, all eager and willing to settle old scores, all filled with hatred of the arrogant native priests.

All willing to tear the heart from the Dra Vheera religion and expose it to the critical gaze of the entire Solar System.

Manson paced uneasily about the control room, the permanent magnets in his boots ringing sharply against the floor plates and, watching him, Colin could sense his inward tension.

"Getting scared, Manson?"

"Scared?" Anger touched the captain's features with spots of red then, as he met the calm stare of the big man, he shrugged and slumped into a chair. "Yes," he admitted. "I suppose I am. This is a big thing we're trying to do." He looked curiously at Colin. "What's this all about, anyway? I know what you told me, but somehow it doesn't seem to make sense. Is there something I don't know?"

"Yes." Colin relaxed and fumbled in his pockets for a crumpled package of cigarettes. He shook one out, puffed it into life, and offered the packet to the captain. Manson shook his head, the habit of years preventing him from smoking while in space. The big man grinned and deliberately blew a smoke ring towards the grill of the air conditioners.

"We've plenty of air and what the hell? This tub is on last voyage."

"I guessed that."

"You guessed right."

"What's the plan, Colin? Who was in that auxiliary which rendezvoused with us in space? What am I letting myself in for?"

"The auxiliary?" The big man shrugged. "Let's just say it was my Boss, you don't think that I had money for all this, did you?" He gestured with the cigarette towards the vessel. "Junk though this ship may be, yet it still cost the best part of a million, and to me that's a fortune. Forget the auxillary, Manson, I make no secret of the fact that I'm working for someone, but who it is doesn't concern you." He dragged at the cigarette. "As for the plan? It's simple. We land on Mars, unofficially, of course, they would never permit us to make planetfall if they knew who we were, and that means we can't use the regular spaceport. After we land we disguise ourselves as Martians and join the once-yearly pilgrimage to the temple. Once inside, we photograph what we can, discover all that's possible, and steal anything we can get away with. We leave the temple, march into the desert, and there we get picked up by an unregistered spaceship. Simple."

"Simple as all hell!" Manson glared his contempt. "We'd never get away with it, and you know it. Damn it, man! The temple is lousy with guards!"

"I know that." Colin crushed out the butt of his cigarette and something feral and cold gleamed for a moment in his slate grey eyes. "I'm not suggesting that this is a picnic we're on. You knew what I intended when you agreed to come. I'm holding you to that, Manson, as I'm holding every man aboard to his promise. We're going to break into the temple and break out again. There's no room for argument."

"I'm not backing out, but have you considered all the difficulties? I can speak Martian, but I doubt whether I could fool a native, much less a priest. And what of the Patrol? How are we going to land without discovery?"

"This ship is going to meet with an accident," said Colin quietly. "It's going to crash, explode, and kill everyone aboard—officially that is. What will really happen is that we bail out and rendezvous in the desert. The ship will crash over a thousand miles from where we land." He shrugged. "A regrettable accident, no more, and who will think of suspecting a few harmless natives?" He smiled with a flash of white teeth. "Relax, Manson, I've given this matter a lot of thought and that's the only way we could ever land on Mars without suspicion."

"That's what you think. What of the bodies? The Patrol will investigate, I know that, and spectroscopic analysis of the remains will reveal the lack of human tissue. You don't know how thorough the Patrol is, Colin, I do. They guard Mars better than Earth."

"There will be bodies, enough to satisfy the Patrol." Colin smiled at the puzzled expression on the captain's face. "We are carrying ten bodies, dead paupers from the charity wards, they will take the place of the crew and satisfy the Patrol. I told you that I'd given this matter some thought and I'm not as foolish as you seem to imagine."

"Ten bodies?" Manson nodded. "That should be enough to account for the crew even though we're carrying twice that number." He looked towards the instrument panel as an alarm shrilled and the control room became flooded with a lucid light. "Getting close. That was the preliminary warning. The Patrol will be radioing us soon for identification and flight course."

"You know what to do." Colin rose and stepped towards the door. "We're emigrants from Earth heading for Callisto of the Jovian System. Ask permission to land to affect engine repairs. Tell them the rockets are pitted all to hell, the plates leak, anything, but persuade them we have to land on Mars. They'll have to allow an emergency halt." He jerked open the panel. "While you're doing that I'll brief the men and break out the cargo."

The cargo was packed in thick boxes and the contents belied the heavy stencils on their exteriors. Those stencils and sworn depositions had enabled the crates to pass unquestioned through the customs and Colin wondered again at the power of unlimited wealth which had shut the right eyes at the right time.

Within the boxes was no farming machinery, no tools, no seeds or supplies. There was metal, smoothly fashioned with engineering perfection. There was equipment and a mass of small boxes, skilful disguises based on the expert assessment of the Martian form. There were other things but all, metal and boxes, added to the same thing.

Guns! Weapons of the most modern manufacture. Instruments of destruction and countless charges for the same. The private army had grown teeth! Heavy side-arms there were, flare-barrelled and with swollen firing chambers, deadly Wilson guns each capable of incinerating an animal the size of a horse at close range, and whose tongue of searing energy could fuse sand and turn metal into molten ruin. Colin caressed them with loving hands as he unpacked the forbidden, incredibly expensive weapons from their packing. Other weapons filled the cases, small needlers, slender barrelled high velocity pistols whose tiny slugs would bring immediate death by hydrostatic shock if they struck an unarmoured torso. Squat grenades and smoke bombs, cylinders of anaesthetic gas, even a dismantled Nione gun.

"Strip," he ordered. "Remove everything down to the skin and put on the Martian clothes." He passed out the weapons. "Strap these around your waist and shoulder holsters. Make sure that they're snug."

A man grunted as he stripped and examined the weapons. "Hell! I feel like a walking arsenal. Do we need all these?"

"You want to go without them?" Colin stared coldly at the man. "Maybe we won't have to use them, but if we do, then I'd rather take a few of the Dra Vheera with me before I die. I remember what happened to a friend of mine, or do you think that the natives will slap your wrist and send you home?"

"Sorry." The man tightened a strap and slipped a Wilson gun into a holster. "What next?"

"First we'll distribute the bodies around the ship. After that you'll put on your disguises and I'll check." Picking up some of the clothing from one of the cases Colin donned own weapons and disguise, then, carrying a spare set, went forward to the control room.

The Martians were humanoid in that they had arms, two legs, a single head and the normal number and distribution of organs. But there, all resemblance to the human race ended. Their skulls were hairless and rose to a bony ridge. Their eyes were slanted, their ears pointed, and their mouths were a bloodless gash. Their skin was hard, tough, almost inflexible and their chest development was larger than that of a Terrestrial. Owing to the hard skin their faces were incapable of registering emotion and, due to the lesser gravity, their physical strength was less than that of any Earthman.

Colin wore a head-mask of flexible plastic which entirely hid his features and which, by molding itself to his skin, gave him the appearance of a Martian. Shapeless robes of a desert dweller and flexible gloves to match the long-fingered nailless hands of the natives completed his attire. The Earthman had been replaced by a creature which any other Terrestrial would have sworn was a living, breathing Martian.

"Get changed, Manson." He stared at the startled features of the captain. "It's me, Colin. Hurry up and change now."

He examined the instrument panel as the captain slipped off his uniform and dressed himself in the disguise.

"How long have we got now?"

"They've already contacted us by radio. I told them the story and they've given us permission to land. A Patrol ship will meet us and lead us down."

"Good." Colin stared at the altered figure of the captain and nodded with satisfaction. "Send the ship into a crash orbit and radio that you're out of control. Signal when we're to jump and waste no time in joining us. You've had experience in drop-gear?"

"Yes."

"Good. Then get yourself ready. I'll attend to the men."

A thin whining echoed through the ship as he rejoined the disguised men. All had now donned their weapons and clothes and stood in uneasy tension at the sound of the thin atmosphere whining against the hull.

"Right! Don drop-gear!"

Colin struggled into the transparent coverall and strapped the air-brakes and rocket reactors to his back. Normal parachutes were useless on Mars, the air was too thin, but whirling bladed air-brakes coupled with a small, compact reaction motor served the same purpose. Even so, jumping from a spaceship moving at several hundred miles an hour at a height of well over sixty miles was no easy task.

Again the whispering drone came from the external hull, a thin, mounting whine as the outer plates warmed by friction and began to radiate heat. Again it came, again, and, as a red lamp flashed from an instrument panel against the hull, Colin signalled with his gloved hand.

Eager hands un-dogged a wide hatch and wrung it aside. A second hatch opened and below them, streaming past like a river of sand, the ochre deserts of Mars reflected the light of a setting sun.

"Ready to drop!" He stared at the tight circle of tense-faced men. "Rendezvous when landed. Jump in fives. Stand by!"

The red lamp blinked out and changed to green.

"Now!"

Bodies dropped through the opened hatch, tumbling as they fell towards the waiting planet, spinning a little as the thin air caught their air-brakes, separating as they plummeted down. Five, and five, and five again. Colin stared desperately towards the control room then, as Manson lunged through the panel towards him, stepped through the hatch and into space.

At first it didn't seem like falling. They were too high, moving too fast for the weak gravity of Mars to be immediately apparent. Sky and desert seemed to whirl about him, red and black, both wheeling and merging into a blur of shifting colour. Then, as the thin air caught at the blades of the airbrake, he steadied and began to fall with increasing speed to the red plains below.

Above and to one side of him a tiny figure tumbled while a second, still spinning, hurled down and past his line of vision. The ship, flame spilling from its venturis, had vanished towards the horizon and a second shape, sleek and trim against the red eye of the setting sun, lanced towards it from out of space. The wreck and the Patrol ship which was to have led it down.

Colin grinned, twisting in his harness and staring at the tiny flames springing up below him, the rocket exhausts from the portable reaction motors. He frowned, wondering if they could be seen from the Patrol ship, but the sleek craft continued on it way without altering its flight pattern and he guessed that the crew was too busy watching the abandoned vessel to notice them.

Carefully he ignited his own motors, feeling the straps wrench into his armpits as they sprouted their little tongues of flame, and gradually he slowed his downward speed. To steer the rockets was hard though not impossible, and he swung and jerked as he guided his path towards several little black specks against the sand.

They had already landed, some of them at least, though others still fell towards the waiting dunes below. As he fell Colin searched the surrounding plain for any signs of life, for a lone prospector, a sand car, or even a group of the nomadic Martians who wrested a frugal living from the sparse lichens and seasonal vegetation following the thaw of the ice caps.

He saw nothing. The desert stretched around him, bare and devoid of all natural life. Only the grouped figures of his own men marred the smooth sweep of the ochre sand, and, his fingers firm on the controls of his drop-gear, he kicked and jerked his way towards them.

He landed just as the far horizon flared to the last light of the dying sun and, as he unstrapped his harness, night, quick and cold, dark and savage, swept over the rolling sands of Mars.

CHAPTER FOUR

DESERT JOURNEY

A man had died during the descent. Colin remembered the figure he had seen tumbling past him and felt sick as he stared at the blood-stained pulp lying on the freezing sand. Around him the others clustered, silent and watchful beneath the brilliant heavens, their gloved hands resting on the butts of concealed weapons as they stared over the empty plains.

"We'll have to bury him," said Colin, and now he spoke the sibilant gutturals of the native language. "Dig a grave and bury all the drop-gear with him. Nothing must remain to show that we landed here."

He gestured to Manson and the other officers and squatted down on the sand, a map spread before him, a compass staring up with its illuminated face.

"We're about a hundred miles from the temple, as near as we dared get. The annual pilgrimage takes place six days from now so we have plenty of time. The best thing would be for us to join up with a band of nomads, but there's too much danger in that." He pointed at the map. "Now listen and take notice. The rendezvous point is here, about sixty miles on the other side of the temple, there's a small cairn of stones there as far as I can remember. I picked it because of that. We'll march towards it and bury the Nione gun, it's too big to carry with us, and then march straight towards our destination. I'll be in command. Manson and Freeguard together with Wilner and Barker, will each take charge of a group. Better still, you stay with me, Manson, the others can each take five men. That will give us a good working unit." He stared again at the map and made a check on the compass. "Right. Have they finish that grave yet?"

"Finished." A man came towards them brushing sand from his hands. "What next?"

"We march. I want to cover some mileage before we settle down. For all we know, someone could have seen us drop and be coming to investigate." He folded up the map and thrust it into a pocket. "One more thing. And this applies to all of you." He waited until they had gathered around him. "We're Martians now, and I don't want to hear anyone speak in other than the native language. If you can't speak it then don't speak at all. Walk calmly and with dignity. Don't straggle and don't on any account remove your masks."

"Where's the harm if we do?" A man scratched at the plastic covering his face. "This thing itches and no one can see us in the dark."

"We'll stop off for shaving and rest later on," said Colin. "But I want you all to get used to acting like the natives. Once we get among them we won't have a chance to make more than one mistake. The quicker you get used to those disguises the better and the only way you'll do that is too think and act and imagine that you are a native-born Martian." He stared up at the glittering stars. "Right. Let's get moving."

Progress wasn't easy and the bitter night wind chilled their blood with its sub-zero temperatures. The stars threw a soft light over the desert and the pools of shadow gave some cover, but Colin had the constant impression of watching eyes and creeping menace. Twice he paused, letting the column advance while he lay in cover, his hand gripping the butt of an H.V. pistol, but only silence and darkness rewarded his vigil. After three hours the numbing cold together with the dehydrating effect of the thin air had reduced the column to shivering discomfort and the men began to straggle and stumble as they marched along. Manson whispered his fears to the big man after the fifth hour.

"They're all in, Colin. We have to rest soon."

"I know it." The big man stared at the wheeling stars. "We may as well make camp now. Remember, no talking and no unnecessary movement. I've got the impression that something is following us and I don't like it."

"Natives?"

"I don't know. I think not, there are more creatures out here than just the natives." He frowned back down the way they had come. "Look—take the men up to the top of that dune and let them bed down. I'll await here."

"Want me to keep watch with you?"

"No. You can set guards around the camp and remember, just let them rest, no eating, no talking, no removing of masks. That will have to wait until daylight when we can get warning if anything comes our way."

Manson nodded, hesitated a moment, then had drifted silently into the darkness following the stumbling line of utterly weary men. Colin narrowed his eyes as he tried to peer into the shadows then, the high velocity pistol in hand, settled down to wait.

Minutes passed, slow and tedious, tightening his nerves until he could feel the tension strain at muscles and sinews. Above his head the stars traced their relentless path across the heavens and the thin wind, bitter and chill, numbed his flesh and chilled his blood. Crouched between two hummocks of sand he waited, eyes wide and strained as he peered into the darkness, the weapon in his hand pointing its slender barrel down the path along which they had come.

Five minutes passed, ten, fifteen, and still the shadows remained harmless pools of darkness and the soft light of the stars revealed no living thing. Almost the big man gave up. Almost he managed to ignore the prickling of primeval warning which told him of alien eyes watching and of an alien presence in the star-shot night. Then...

It came with a rustling motion over the gritty sand. Like a moving patch of darkness, long, sinuous, its legs a weaving blur, its snout lowered to the sand, its mandibles wide and, poised over its ebon shell, its stinger aimed and ready for any unwary prey. A terth. A creature which lived deep in the sand, half-insect, half-plant, big brother to the innumerable sand-lice, a thing which hunted its prey by their warmth and the water content of their bodies.

A creature often used by the nomadic tribes for tracking and in that, similar to the dogs of Earth.

Colin sucked in his breath as he saw it and his hand tightened around the butt of his gun. Tightened, then relaxed again. A Wilson gun would incinerate the creature in a puff of incandescence leaving only smoking ash. A high velocity gun would rip it apart, the tiny slugs exploding against its shell as they vented their enormously kinetic energy in furious heat. But both energy weapons and pistol would make a noise—and the terth need not be alone!

It weaved closer, its mandibles picking up the animal scent from the gritty sand and, watching it, the big man thrust away the pistol and drew his knife. He had to stop it before it reached the camp for there its sting would wreak havoc among the helpless men and, even if one should shoot it, such a noise could mean discovery and the end of their hopes. Tensing, Colin gripped the knife and, as the horrible scorpion-like thing hesitated opposite him, he flung himself out and forward.

Chitin moved beneath his hands and the sting lashed him with stunning force. He dodged, stabbed, slashed with the keen edge, wrenched with his hands and kicked with his heavy boots. Liquid sprayed around him, the poison from the severed stinger, and thin legs scrabbled at the sand as the crippled insect tried to use its inoperative sting. Inoperative merely because it could no longer sting and paralyse, but dangerous with its hammer blows, too dangerous.

Colin grunted as it slammed against his shoulder, thrust desperately with the knife at overlapping segments of shell, smashed thin legs to broken ruin with his heavy boots, and snatched his hand away from gnashing mandibles. Dust rose around them, a thin, choking cloud of drifting particles, and the terth ripped his robe to shreds with its hooked limbs. Again the big man stabbed, again, a third time, bearing down on the thin blade and crushing the ebon chitin with desperate blows. Abruptly the terth stiffened, seemed almost to arc its back in a circle, then, as green fluids gushed from its ripped abdomen, toppled and fell in a crumpled ruin.

Breathing heavily, Colin staggered to his feet, the knife a green-tinged talon in his hand, and automatically he wiped it and slid it back into its sheath. The terth was dead, its inner juices spilled onto the hungry sand, and already the tiny bodies of the sand-lice, the scavengers of Mars, were busy ripping it to shreds and carrying it away to their nests.

Within a couple of hours there would be no trace of either the insect or its blood.

Manson rose as he staggered into the camp, treading carefully around the slumped figures of the sleeping men, and the grizzled captain peered anxiously at him in the brilliant starlight.

"A terth," explained Colin grimly. "I knifed it."

"Knifed it!" Manson pursed his lips as he saw the condition of the big man's robe. "Did it sting?"

"Would I be here now if it had?" Colin winced as he sat down. "I severed the sting but I couldn't prevent it hitting me with the stump."

"Then you're bruised." Manson fumbled among his clothing. "Get that robe off, never mind the cold, this salve will prevent stiffness." He thinned his lips as he rubbed the soothing paste over the big man's torso. "Hell! You look as if you'd been flogged with a sledge-hammer."

"I feel it too." Colin looked ruefully at the torn robe. "We'll have to bury this. Luckily we've got a couple of spares." He sighed and rested his aching head on a pillow of sand. "Wake me at dawn."

Dawn came with fair promise, a gentle growth of pink and gold, of orange and amber, washing the ochre desert with pastel shades as the sun rose with slow majesty above the oddly near horizon. Warmth came with the sun, driving away the freezing chill of night and restoring jaded spirits with its gentle touch. Colin woke as the sunlight touched his face and lay for a moment, collecting his thoughts, wondering why he should be stiff and sore. Memory returned and he was on his knees, his eyes searching the desert, his breath clogging his throat with sudden panic.

Nothing. The desert was bare of any living thing, and he sighed and relaxed as he realised that the terth must have been alone.

"Manson!" He pointed to a ring of low dunes a few hundred yards away. "Place men on these points and tell them to keep close watch. The rest will eat and shave, we can't let our beards grow beneath the face-masks; no Martian known has ever been seen to scratch his chin." He turned as men slipped to the observation points and woke the rest. "Freeguard! Collect rations and warm energised soup. The rest of you get those masks off and clean up. Hurry, now!"

He set the pace, stripping off the mask, smearing depilatory cream over his stubble and wiping off both cream and chemically-removed hairs. The mask back over his head he arranged for the food, rich, warm, highly energised soup gulped out of self-heating cans. Then, the watchers replaced and fed, the debris buried, he gave orders for the march.

"Keep close now. We should reach the cairn by nightfall and there we can bury the Nione and get ready for the final step. Same orders as before and watch your step. Martians don't take such long strides as we do." He stared at them and the sibilant gutturals of the native language slipped from between his almost motionless lips beneath the grotesque head-mask.

"You're Martians now, and don't forget it. Unless you can learn the part before we reach the temple, we'll all die. Today I'll be watching you and the man who lets us down will know it. None of you are strangers to the planet, nearly all of you can understand if not speak the language, and you know how the nomad tribes act and behave. Remember that. One mistake can lead to all our deaths. March now, we'll discuss final plans later. Ready? March!"

Silently the file of men moved into the flowing light of the Martian day.

Gradually as they walked, the last vestiges of Earth fell away from them. Colin walked beside them, his hard eyes alert for the slightest error, and from his ten years' experience he knew just how the Martians should appear. To Terrestrial eyes, of course, he had no way of knowing whether or not their disguise would fool a native. But they walked right, looked right, had dispensed with all the trivial gestures with which the normal Earthman was afflicted, and as they progressed through the day, he knew that they were as near to the real thing as they could hope to be.

The test came just before evening when the last light of the setting sun threw long shadows across the rolling dunes.

A speck grew on the horizon, a dun-coloured speck against the dun-coloured sand, almost invisible as it descended below the sky line but Colin knew what it must be. He forged ahead, taking his place at the front of the marching column and, just as the upper segment of the sun showed above the horizon, the speck reappeared as a full grown native.

He paused as he saw them, waiting with the calm, almost incredible patience of his race and, as Colin came abreast, greeted him in the stilted, almost archaic language of ancient Mars.

"The day is well for traveling."

"It is well." Colin sweated beneath his mask and resisted the impulse to grip his pistol. For the first time he felt how hopeless their quest was going to be. He knew the polite forms of conversation but if the man should make some religious gesture, some phrase connected with the Dra Vheera…

"You travel perhaps to the temple?" The word wasn't "temple" and it didn't mean just that, but "temple" was the nearest any Terrestrial could come to the half-worshipful half-reverent expression used to denote the centre of the Dra Vheera cult. Semanticists had worn themselves thin trying to discover just what many of the Martian words really meant and any Earthman speaking the language still operated on a large percentage of guesswork.

"We do."

"You have journeyed far?"

"From the regions far to the west. You will accept water?" Colin knew that he was on safe ground here. It was custom to offer guests water and any group smaller than your own were automatically considered guests. It was also the custom to refuse such an offer unless there was dire need, for on Mars water was far more precious than gold.

"My thanks for your offer and my regret that I must refuse." The sibilant gutturals hung on the thin air as the native made the ritual refusal. "I must not detain you. The way is long and the perils many. May Dra Vheera watch and comfort you."

He made a particular gesture, a circular pattern with the extended forefinger of his right hand, nodded, and like a shadow among shadows had vanished into the night. Not until Colin had put at least three miles between them did he relax. Manson joined him as they strode ahead.

"Learn anything, Colin?"

"We passed, superficially at least, but I had a bad moment when he mentioned religion. You notice the gesture?"

"Like this?" The captain weaved his right forefinger through the air. "I got it. Maybe we should learn it, it seems to be some sort of custom between them, like a special grip between lodge members back home."

"Yes." Colin shivered a little at the first bite of the night wind. "We can't really assume that because he didn't seem to notice that we were different others won't. He could be pretty low on the social and intelligence level, relative to the natives I mean. After all, if we were on Earth and met a desert wanderer or an agricultural worker, we wouldn't think that he was a representative member of the entire civilisation. The real intelligence's are all in the priesthood and they are the ones we have to be careful of."

"I've been thinking," said Manson abruptly. "What would you have done had he discovered us?"

"Do?" Colin didn't alter the level tone of his voice but the captain nodded as if he had learned the answer to his question.

"I thought so. There's big money tied up in this thing, isn't there?"

"Yes. If we get what the Boss wants, then we'll all be rich—those of us that are left alive, that is."

"You expect trouble?"

"We're armed, aren't we?" Colin didn't look towards the disguised figure at his side. "We carry portable radios tuned to a sealed beam. We have enough equipment take a city and our fire-power could destroy a regiment of any old-time army. This isn't a picnic, Manson."

"I didn't think that it was, but..." The captain swallowed. "To shoot down an innocent native just because he might have known who we were. I don't like it, Colin."

"We didn't shoot him."

"But you would have done had he known."

"Perhaps, but I didn't and so there's no need for you to get upset." The big man didn't alter his stride but his voice hardened as he returned to his own language. "Listen, Manson. All of us are walking a tight-rope with certain death if we miss our footing. If the natives don't get us and torture us, the Patrol will arrest us and hand us over to the Dra Vheera. We're outlaws. We can't rely on anyone but ourselves and the guns we carry. This is war, a private and personal war between us and the forces of two planets. If we win, then we shall be rich and safe. If we lose, then we shall be dead, or worse than dead. It is as simple as that. Do you think that one life, whether native or Terrestrial can matter now? Get some sense, man! It's too late to back out now."

"You're insane, Colin. Both you and this mysterious Boss of yours. I wish…"

"You wish that you were still rotting in that flea-bit hotel where I found you?" The big man shrugged. "I warned you what I was after and you agreed to take the risk. There's big money at the end of it, money and a safe passage to Venus or the Outer Worlds where we can enjoy it without question. I want that money and I want to pay back this damn planet for all it's done to me. I'm going to do it, Manson! I'm going do it if I have to convert the temple to molten ruin and blast the entire priesthood into smoking ash!"

"Yes," said the captain quietly. "I think that you would."

"I would." Colin laughed and slipped back into Martian as he squeezed the captain's arm. "Cheer up, man! The hard part is behind us. We landed without discovery, passed an actual test with a living native, and all we have to do now is to mingle with the pilgrims and enter the temple. We may not even have to fire a single shot. We may be able to walk in and out without question. A week from now you may be remembering the whole episode as something to tell your children. Stop worrying. Just remember what the Dra Vheera did to you, did to all of us, and then you won't get cold feet at the thought of a little killing." Colin peered through the starlit night.

"There's the cairn, see? That heap of stones over there. There's a canal nearby and we aren't more than three days march from the Temple."

Silently he led the way to the shapeless bulk looming against the stars.

CHAPTER FIVE

WITHIN THE TEMPLE

The temple of Dra Vheera was a man-made mountain soaring high above the rolling dunes of the ochre desert. From a wide base it rose in delicate curves to a towering pinnacle, a fresco of turrets and spires, of arches and strange angles, convoluted and writhing in alien patterns of stone. Old it was, so old that all the intricate carvings and bas-reliefs which had once covered its surface had long since been worn away by the whining storms and abrasive sand. Now it stood, polished by age and shimmering beneath the light of a distant sun, enigmatic, mysterious, the centre and home of a planetary religion.

Around it, stretching in a ten-mile circle, was the forbidden zone, an area of desert on which no Earthman was allowed to tread, while above it, stretching far into space, was another, invisible, intangible zone was barred to all aircraft and spaceships. It rested there as it had rested for unguessable eons and, even though Mars now held two races, one of then the most insatiably curious known, still it retained its mystery.

Colin stared up at it from where he stood at the edge of the forbidden zone, staring at the distant pinnacle, all that could be seen above the horizon. Around him the other disguised Terrestrials clustered as though for mutual support and around them, moving in small, silent groups over the entire desert, the natives moved with stately tread towards the object of their once-yearly pilgrimage.

"This is it," said Colin, and though he mouthed the words no word passed his lips. The tiny throat-mike caught his words by conduction and sent them over the sealed-beam radios each man carried. "We've passed so far and there's no reason to think that we're going to be caught. Advance in groups and we'll meet up inside. No talking, no using the radio unless essential, and above all, no wild shooting."

"What's the plan once we're inside?" The whispering voice echoed from the button-speaker behind his ear and the big man frowned as he tried to identify the questioner.

"I've told you that before. The officers will photograph anything of interest and some of you will record the sound of their ritual, if any. Don't act on your own volition. Any looting to be done will be done at my orders. If we have to start shooting, then fire quick and often. If we become separated, you all know the rendezvous point and the ship will arrive exactly four days from now. Right. No more questions now. Here we go!" Steadily he led the way forward over the gritty sand, walking as the natives walked, thankful that the shapeless robes hid the differences of his body. The other followed him, wending their way in three little groups towards the distant pinnacle of the temple.

One mile and nothing had happened. The natives were a trifle more numerous, a shade nearer to each other as they headed towards a common point, but that was all.

Five miles, half-way through the forbidden zone, and ahead of them the temple seemed to have grown higher out of the ground, only the wide base remaining hidden below the horizon. Colin began to sweat and cursed the plastic hugging his skin.

Seven miles and the impulse to stop and stare, to gather the others around him, to march as a unit, weapons in hands in their advance towards the temple, became almost irresistible. Grimly he walked on, his stride never faltering, and before him the monstrous temple grew even larger.

Nine miles and now the natives were thick around him. Hundreds of them, thousands, all walking steadily forward, not looking anywhere but at the temple, not speaking, seeming almost robot-like in their rapt concentration. Colin tried to imagine that he walked among a normal crowd but the differences were too great. Here there was no whispering, no curious or excited expressions, no flurry of activity or change of posture. Here was only silence and the steady scuff of marching feet.

Ten miles—and he stood before the temple!

Doors pierced it, huge, double-leaved doors breaking the smooth surface of the exterior at regular intervals. Through those doors the natives marched with hesitation and, gritting his teeth, Colin headed towards the one opposite to him. Martians stood in a circle around the base of the temple. Tall, their eyes smouldering pits of green fire in their hairless skulls, and the crest of each was stained a brilliant yellow to match their robes.

"Space!" The whisper seemed a shout against the big man's ear. "Priests! Thousands of them!"

"Silence!" Colin forced himself not to stare at the watchful ranks of the Dra Vheera priesthood. "Keep your hands in plain sight and don't hesitate."

Tensely he led the way towards the black mouth of the open door.

It was dark inside and fear crawled over his nerves as the blackness closed around him. How good were the Martian defences? On Earth it would have been a simple matter to rig devices to scan the incoming crowds. Electronic equipment would have shown the presence of metal, the subtle radiations from the energy weapons, shown the alien bone structure and humidity index. Here? He almost grunted with relief as he stepped into a soft green luminescence. Experts or not the priests hadn't installed modern equipment. He was inside the temple!

For a moment the temptation to stop and stare was almost too great them, as he remembered where he was and what would happen if they were discovered, he forced himself to move from the door and into the swirling green luminescence. It was like a thin fog, a thin, green mist, and tiny sparkles hung in the emerald glow like unwinking eyes or trapped stars caught in the web of some unguessable spider. It drifted around him, shielding him from view and making the half-seen forms of others blur and shift as though seen through water or through distorting glass. Then he was through the green mist, stepping into a tremendous hall of whispering stone and around him shone a soft blue radiance stemming from the very walls themselves.

He paused then, following the example of the other figures around him, the tall, calm-eyed figures of natives and, watching them, Colin felt an easing of his fear. Not all of them had been here before.

It was obvious in the way they stood, their eyes glinting emerald against the sapphire, their heads moving as they scanned the soaring walls and the incredibly vast hall. Behind him Colin felt the other Earthman pass through the green mist and cluster at his back. A voice whispered in his ear.

"What next?"

"Take it easy. Notice those natives, see how they stare, I'll bet that this is the first time any of them have been here."

"Impossible! This is a yearly pilgrimage."

"Perhaps. But if I'm right, it makes things a lot easier for us. Watch now! There's a priest!"

A tall figure dressed all in brilliant yellow crossed towards them on soundless feet. He paused before the natives and Colin caught their whispered syllables.

"Dra Vheera welcomes you. For the first time?"

"We are so honoured."

"May your visits be many. Follow the red line and an acolyte will attend you." The priest made the curious gesture Colin had seen before, an intricate weaving of his extended forefinger. The native returned the gesture and walked steadily along a thin, red line on the blue limned flooring.

"Dra Vheera welcomes you. For the first time?"

"We are so honoured." Colin gave mental thanks to whatever Gods of luck had taken charge of him that he had already learned the obvious formula.

"May your visits be many," intoned the priest and repeated the directions. Colin returned his symbolic gesture, guessing that the native was too busy greeting the new arrivals to pay much attention.

"What now?" He guessed that the whispering voice came from Manson, but the conduction radio distorted normal tones to a flat drone.

"We follow the red line and some other priest will attend us."

"You think we should?"

"Why not? The quicker we get into things the better. Follow me now."

The red line led straight to a low booth and ended against another belt of the green mist. Colin slowed as he approached, watching those who had gone before, then swung to one side as he saw what they were doing. As each native reached the booth an attendant priest guided his arm into a slot at the side of an unfamiliar machine. A needle kicked on a wide dial and, after withdrawing his arm, the native passed on into and supposedly through the second belt of emerald fog.

What the machine was Colin couldn't guess, but he knew that whatever it was, they had to avoid it. Deliberately, he led the way towards the circling vapour.

Within the belt were the Martians.

They squatted on the blue-lit floor, thousands of them, sitting perfectly motionless in serried rows, their heads all facing towards the centre where a great globe of some shimmering material floated without obvious means of support. Priests moved among them, silent shapes in brilliant yellow, and over priests and worshippers hung an eerie silence. Silently Colin led the way towards the assembled natives and, following their example, squatted tailor-fashion, on the warm stone.

"I don't like this." Again the big man guessed it was Manson who spoke. "What are these natives supposed to be doing?"

"This could be a service of some kind," breathed Colin impatiently. "Remember that we are dealing with an alien religion and their form of worship may have nothing in common with our own."

"I don't see that. All religions follow the same basic pattern. There should be an object of worship, an idol, a symbol, anything to centre the attentions and form a focal point. The only thing I can see here is that globe. And where are the priests conducting the service? Where is the ritual, the pattern? As far as I can see we are just waiting for nothing."

"Shut up, Manson." Colin guessed by the sudden inhalation that he had guessed correctly. "Impatience now could ruin everything. Relax and take it easy. This has been a lot simpler than I hoped."

"Perhaps," said the captain gloomily. "We haven't tried to get out yet."

Colin didn't answer.

Time passed with leaden feet, dragging, moving as if a second had become an hour, an hour eternity. The unfamiliar posture began to send pain darting through cramped muscles and still nothing appeared to be happening to the assembled throng. Colin watched the softly moving priests, the shimmering ball floating high above their heads, the ranked, incredibly motionless array of natives, and began to wish that he had never led the way directly into the central gathering.

It would have been wiser to have skirted the vast hall. There should have been stairs somewhere leading to the upper regions, to the personal apartments of the priests and the archives of the temple. Here was nothing except what the priesthood chose to show to the masses, and Colin was cynical enough not to have any illusions about religion. To him it was superstition. He began to look around him, slowly, cautiously, and yet, because of the ease with which they had penetrated the temple, with increasing carelessness.

The crowd seemed to have reached stability, no fresh figures came through the green belt of luminous vapour and the priests had ceased their constant movement between the rows of silent figures. Colin guessed that the service, if service it was, had about to begin and he leaned forward a little to ease his cramped bones.

With shocking abruptness, the hovering globe flared with brilliant light then, even as the big man blinked to drive away the retinal after-images, it flowed with ever-changing colour. It was wonderful, that colour. It merged and blended in a shifting pattern of iridescence, hue after hue mingling and changing in kaleidoscopic brilliance. An undreamed orchestra of transmuted music, a symphony of light, a weaving melody of pure colour.

"Don't look at it." The drone hummed against the big man's ear. "Colin! Don't look at it!"

"Yes." Colin bit his lips beneath the mask and, closing his eyes, relayed swift instructions. "Close your eyes. Keep your heads turned towards the globe but close your eyes. That thing's hypnotic and dangerous. Freeguard! Barker! Swanson! All of you! Don't look at that globe!"

Easily said but not easily done. Even through closed eyelids Colin could sense the rippling surge of colour and he had to fight the impulse to open his eyes and stare at the resplendent beauty of the thing. It seemed to last a long time, the silence, the washing flow of brilliance, the tense hush over the assembled natives. Then words spilled from the air, the sibilant gutturals of the Martian tongue, seeming to speak to each person individually as they ebbed through the incredible stillness.

"Dra Vheera bids you welcome. Dra Vheera is happy that you are here for Dra Vheera is you and you are Dra Vheera. Relax now, ease yourselves into the One for this is our time as it was, and as it shall be."

"Colin!" Manson's voice throbbed over the radio. "Listen!"

"I'm listening. Is the recorder working?"

"It's working," said another voice sleepily. "I'm getting it all."

"Watch yourself," snapped the big man. "Don't let that globe put you under." He focused his attention on the sibilant voice.

"This is the creed of Dra Vheera. This is your creed and mind, our creed and that of those who have gone before. We are one. The individual is all and all is the individual. We are one. The race is all and we are the race. We are one."

Colin bit his lips as the hypnotic repetition of syllables tore at his awareness. It would be so easy to sleep, so easy, so easy... He jerked awake as the speaker droned behind his ear.

"Look at them, Colin! Look at them!"

"Don't look at them. Close your eyes and keep them closed. Guard yourself!"

Again he tasted blood as his teeth chewed at his lip and again he concentrated on what the solitary voice was saying.

"...and so, once every cycle, those of us who are prepared assemble here to make the supreme gesture for the good of all. But it is not death. There is no death while the race survives and there can be no individual death while the future is an unread scroll. Into our hands those who go leave themselves and into our hands they leave their life and awareness. It will not be for long. Now that our home has felt the tread of alien feet, it will not be for long. Dra Vheera will restore the lost seas and gardens. Dra Vheera will renew the racial vigour. Dra Vheera is all and all is one."

A sigh broke free from the assembled Martians. An exhalation of pent-up breath, the first sound Colin had heard since he had joined them and, subtly, the tension seemed to increase. Deliberately he opened his eyes, careful not to stare at the resplendent ball of shifting colour, and his thumb brushed the switch which sent micro-film spinning through the camera strapped to his chest.

"Now is the hour for the Chosen! Now is the time of giving and of receiving. Some will go that others may remain and yet, to those who go, let them be comforted in the knowledge that they will awaken again. Let this be your comfort and your guard. The aliens who pollute our world will not reign for long. Dra Vheera will vanquish them. Their own desires will undo them. They are as savages beneath our eyes. Speak not to them. Explain nothing to them. Ignore them. They are animals and you are Dra Vheera. There can be no unity of minds between us and they. Tell them nothing of Dra Vheera. Tell them nothing of Dra Vheera. Tell them nothing of Dra Vheera."

The lambent globe shifted, swung, circled slowly above the uplifted faces then drifted to a stop. A finger of searing purple light stabbed down from it, a shaft of eye-twisting brilliance and where a Martian had sat, eyes focussed in rapt concentration on the globe, there was nothing. Nothing but a smear of ash, a tiny heap of grey dust and something which looked like a tiny, glittering gem. For a moment it rested there, winking in the soft blue light then, flashing like a burning meteor, it lifted from the floor and darted towards the barrier of green mist. It struck, merged, and within an incredibly brief space of time was one with the other points of gleaming brilliance trapped in the emerald fog.

Again the globe drifted, seemingly at random, and again the purple shaft flashed silent destruction. Again the ash and the glittering gem, the streak of light and the strange merging of the brilliant speck in its green setting. Again. Again. Time after time and, as the purple light flashed and natives crumpled into dust, a strange energy began to pervade the green-edged area. It was something like the tension Colin had experienced during a storm, a sense of strain, as if electrical forces were warring in sub-etheric dimensions. A tingling pervaded his nerves and the short hairs on the back of his neck lifted in primeval reflex to unknown dangers.

Again the globe drifted and the purple lightning flashed. Again and again, and, as it drifted and paused and drifted again, Colin kept silent count of the natives who vanished beneath the lash of its alien ray. Fifty! A hundred! A hundred and fifty! Two hundred! A pause, a hesitation, then, almost reluctantly it seemed, the globe returned to its original position and the flaring colours on its surface died to a shimmering flow.

"It's over!" The tiny voice against his ear roused Colin to instant awareness. "For a moment there I thought it that it was heading towards us."

"Steady, Manson. Rouse the others and let's get moving."

Dimly he heard the captain's voice snap orders to the rest of the men then, slowly and carefully, following the example of the natives, he rose and stretched his limbs. One by one the Terrestrials joined him, silent and thoughtful, tense and nervous, their hands unconsciously straying towards the butts of their hidden guns, their stance that of men ready to meet immediate danger.

Abruptly the green mist writhed away from the central portion, recoiling back to the edge of the vast hall where it merged with the first belt of emerald fog. Priests stood where the barrier had been. Tall natives, dressed all in yellow, their tinted crests odd in the blue radiance. They moved among the natives, whispering, touching their shoulders, making strange gestures with their long fingers, shepherding the worshippers at the strange ceremony to one side of the great hall.

For a moment Colin stood in doubt, not knowing just what to do next, then, as yellow robed priest headed towards him, he strode towards the distant wall.

Three paces he took, three long strides, then halted with his nerves tingling with the instinct of approaching danger.

"Colin!" The word droned against his ear. "Behind us!"

There were five of them, tall, yellow-dressed, their face expressionless, their long-fingered hands empty of weapons. They stared at the little group of disguised Earthman and Colin moved towards them as if to speak with the priests of Dra Vheera as the other worshippers had done. He didn't have a chance. The central priest, one who bore a peculiar red insignia on the front of his robe, spoke first.

"Welcome to Dra Vheera," he said quietly. "May good fortune attend you."

The words were harmless, a simple formula, more than anything else but they filled Colin with a sick of what was to come.

For they were spoken in flawless Terran.

CHAPTER SIX

THE GREEN MIST

Even then Colin fought to maintain the deception. The priest could be suspicious, he could guess, but he couldn't know, and Colin wasn't going to betray himself out of his own mouth. So he stared blankly at the yellow-garbed figure and stammered in the sibilant gutturals of the native tongue.

"Dra Vheera attend you. I..."

"Please." Ancient courtesy dictated the stilted words but feral hate glowed in the green eyes of the priest. "To continue this farce would be a waste of time. It may interest you to learn that you were discovered on entering the temple. However, as an assembly was in process of formation, it was decided to wait until now." The bloodless lips twitched in a gesture akin to a sneer. "Even then you were so terribly obvious. During the assembly we could sense that you were not absorbing and you had not even registered as new arrivals. I..."

The needler made little sound, a muffled thud, less noise than that of a man snapping his fingers and the metabolism of Martian and Terrestrial was close enough for the darts to take instant effect. The priest blinked, staggered a little, and before he had slumped to the blue-limned stone his companions had joined him in drugged unconsciousness.

"Let's get out of here!" Panic made the captain's voice throb over the radio. "Someone may have seen..."

"They have." Colin stared grimly at the advancing figures of yellow-robed priests then looked about him. At their feet the five Martians lay slumped in drugged helplessness. Around them in a rapidly thickening circle the priests advanced with steady pace, their eyes green against the blue radiance, their hands as yet empty of weapons. Above their heads the vast hall lost itself in a blue haze while around them, creeping at the heels of the yellow-robed figures, the peculiar gem-studded green mist surged like a leashed fog. Of native Martians other than the priests there was no sign.

For a moment Colin was tempted. A single energy weapon would incinerate the priests into smoking ash and the entire temple would be theirs for loot and study. It seemed hard to have done so much, to have come so far, and reaped so little reward. Barnhart wouldn't be pleased. He had expected something concrete, something akin to a sacred relic, some clue as to what the Dra Vheera cult was all about. He would disappointed—and he had the money.

"We could take the priests," suggested Manson, the needle gun reflecting the blue luminescence as he gestured towards them. "Use them as hostages."

"No." Colin gauged the distance of the advancing priests. Their slow advance worried him as did the enigmatic curtain of green mist billowing behind them and shielding everything but the immediate vicinity. "These Martians would have no compunction at killing their own kind." He frowned as he stared about the deserted area of the vast hall. If there were only something they could take with them, some object, something to satisfy Barnhart and explode the Dra Vheera cult, he would be more satisfied. As it was, even if they escaped, and there seemed no reason why they shouldn't be able to shoot their way to safety, it would have been a wasted journey.

Abruptly he made up his mind.

"Right! Action stations. Use needlers and follow me."

Deliberately he ran towards the yellow line, the little weapon in his hand sending a spray of tiny darts before him, darts which should have crumpled the priests to slumped helplessness as they had the other five. Behind him ran the others, all nineteen of them shooting as they ran, a hurtling mass of grimly determined men armed and desperate. The Martians should have wavered, should have fallen or run, should have broken rank and yielded to the charge.

They didn't.

They stood, motionless, their slanted eyes and hairless skulls looking like masks in the dim light and around them the green mist swirled as though imbued with a life of its own. Then, from somewhere above and behind them, purple lightning lanced towards the men of Earth.

A man screamed and fell and rolled shrieking on the blue stone. Another cursed as the gun melted in his hand, then tore frantically at concealed weapons, to shrivel in searing death as their charges exploded in lurid frenzy. A third whined and clapped his hands to blinded eyes.

"Back!" Colin swore as he dropped his needler and tugged at the twin butts of Wilson guns. "Back for your lives!"

Thunder ripped the silence and lancing tongues of destruction reached from the orifices of his weapons as he squeezed the triggers. Yellow robes vanished in flaming ruin, the green mist shuddered and recoiled as though cruelly hurt, and suddenly the way was clear before them. Again he fired, again, and now other weapons added their roar of destruction to those he carried. Hunched together the remaining Earthman raced desperately past the curtain of emerald fog and headed towards the gaping arch of a door.

They never made it. Even as they ran towards it the great portal swung shut and purple fire winked from a point from the right. Colin answered the menacing glow with bolts of shattering energy then desperately looked around for some means of escape. He no longer thought of loot, of something to prove what they had done and where they had been. Money was useless to a dead man and now that the Dra Vheera were alerted their lives hung on a thread. It was time to get out—and fast!

"Where are they?" Manson almost choked with panic as he stared around the deserted hall. "That mist, it's following us. Colin!"

"Steady!" The big man narrowed his eyes as he glanced around. The captain was right. The surging curtain of emerald, gem-shot mist was closing around them barring all escape. Unless…

Purple lightning struck at him as he stepped towards the weaving curtain, his guns automatically answering the writhing menace. He stepped back just in time, then deliberately triggered his weapons as he sent shaft after shaft of searing destruction directly towards the shielding mist. Behind him the men had fallen into position, their guns ready to lay a barrage of flame as soon as they had a target, but there was no target, nothing but green mist and the hidden projector of the purple ray.

Suddenly Colin had the impression that they were at the mercy of the Dra Vheera.

He didn't like it. He didn't like the mystery, the silence, the lack of natives. He felt his skin crawl as though he were being watched by a million unseen eyes and sweat made his face a streaming discomfort beneath the mask.

"They're playing with us," he snapped. "Well, maybe we'll give them something to play with." He jerked a grenade from his belt. "Let's see how they like this." Carefully he threw the small container of compressed energy into the green mist then flung himself flat to avoid the concussion.

It came with a roar of echoing sound, a blast of air and a rolling thunder. Together with the explosion came a brittle sound, a crystalline tinkling as of shattering glass, and an impression, more emotional than physical, made his senses reel with sudden pain and outraged horror. When he looked up the green mist had parted, was recoiling to either side while the blue stone of the floor was littered with what seemed to be tiny fragments of dull glass.

Beyond the parted curtain stood the priests of the Dra Vheera.

Armed now, their hands filled with strange mechanisms of twisted metal and convoluted crystal, while before them, squat and ugly, stood what could only be the projector of the purple ray. Even as he saw it the guns thundered in Colin's hands and other shafts of energy lanced from others. One bolt the projector fired. One writhing streamer of purple flame, then it blossomed into flaming luminescence and a cloud of scintillant particles hovered in expanding glory where it had stood.

But it had done serious damage.

Five men had died in writhing agony beneath the touch of the ray and two others whimpered as they saw what had happened to their bodies. Colin swore as he looked around him. Ten men out of action, half their number, and they hadn't even started to escape yet. Manson crawled towards him, his Wilson gun spouting energy at the scuttling shapes of the distant priests.

"What now, Colin? We can't get through the doors and those priests will be back soon."

"I know it." The big man lifted himself and stared over the deserted expanse of the hall. The green mist had recoiled to a point far off and the priests seemed to have vanished. "That grenade must have upset them. Good. Now to get out of this rat-trap."

"There's a stairway over there." The captain pointed with the gun in his hand. "See? Over by that buttress. If we could make it we'd stand a better chance. We're sitting ducks here."

"I know it." Colin rose to his feet then ducked as a coiling serpent of green fire twisted towards him. "Cover me, Manson. The devils are sniping." He stood upright as the captain fired at a point on the wall and scanned the immediate surroundings. No priests, no projectors, no mist. He dropped flat again and spoke into the throat mike. "Listen. There's a stairway over to the right. We can make it and once under cover we'll have a better chance. We'll have to make it fast and smooth. Cross-fire and shoot at anything that moves. I'll give the word when to move."

"What about the wounded?" Manson glanced towards the injured men. "Can we take them with us?"

"No."

"But why not? We..."

"I said, no!" Colin's voice was harsh as he snapped the word. "They knew what they faced and they would only hamper us. They stay behind."

"You devil!"

"Shut up. Get ready to move. Now!"

As one man they leapt to their feet and followed Colin as he ran towards the narrow slit of the stairway. Energy reached towards them from scattered points from the looming walls, coiling serpents of green fire, sapphire stars of frigid coldness, ruby beams of blistering hear. They answered the fire, their weapons spouting a continuous stream of thundering destruction and, incredibly, they made it safe to the narrow stair and plunged upwards into unknown regions.

Colin led the way, his overworked guns blistering his fingers through his plastic gloves, and broke gasping into a small room at the head of the stairs. Quickly he ran through the small chamber and slammed a door, thrusting a chest against the thick wooden portal. Only then did he relax.

"Right. Check and reload your weapons." Irritably he stripped the mask from his sweating features and peeled the gloves from his hands. "These things won't do us much good now, but don't throw them away, we might still find a use for them." He stepped to the head of the stairs and listened. "Nothing down there, but they would be fools to try a frontal attack. Barker!"

"Barker's dead, he got his in the second blast." A man winced as he nursed a burned arm.

"Freeguard?"

"Here."

"Good. Take a man and guard these stairs. Manson!"

"Yes?"

"Come over here." Colin squatted down as the captain joined him and deliberately disconnected his throat mike. "This is between us two. Uncouple your mike."

"Right." Manson pulled free the connection and stared at the big man. "Well?"

"We're in trouble, bad trouble." Colin grunted as he thrust fresh charges into his still-hot weapons. "Those priests surprised me, who'd have thought that they had energy weapons? We should have been able to burn our way without trouble. Damn them! Ten men gone and for what?"

"Don't you know?"

"No. That's what annoys me. All this trouble and nothing to show for it. What did you make of the ceremony?"

"Nothing." Manson shrugged at the big man's expression. "Some things are obvious, of course. The hypnotism, the post-hypnotic suggestions that the natives should tell us nothing of Dra Vheera, the insistence that the individual is the race and that the race is the individual. I followed that enough but I couldn't make out the sacrifices or what they were. Another thing, did you see those gems lift and dart towards the green mist?"

"Yes."

"Good. I wondered if it was just me or it really happen." Manson frowned and shook his head. "One thing is certain, the Martians aren't the ignorant peasants we took them for."

"You can say that again." Colin snapped shut the loading chambers of his weapons and thrust them into their holsters. "Their use of energy weapons proves that. Another thing, did you notice how the needlers failed when we charged? And that green fog?" He thinned his lips as he remembered the way the emerald curtain had hemmed them in. "It was almost as if they could control the damn thing. Like an electronic barrier which absorbed or deflected the darts. I wonder…"

Thunder rolled from the head of the stairs and Freeguard yelled an urgent warning.

"They're coming!"

"Burn them down!" Colin half-rose then relaxed as the engineer grinned back at him and made a gesture with his thumb and forefinger.

"Relax! I got 'em, you concentrate on getting us out of here." Grimly he returned to his task of blasting creeping shapes to smoking ash. Manson stared at the big man.

"He's right. How do we get out?"

"I don't know." Colin jerked to the roar of the Wilson guns. "One thing's certain, we're in a hell of a mess. Maybe we aren't all going to make it. Maybe some of us will have to stay behind to cover the rest." He stared sombrely towards where the engineer fired from the head of the narrow stairs. "We're like rats up here. Trapped. And sooner or later those priests are going to think of using gas." He snapped his fingers. "Gas! That's it! We can make a break for it under cover of the smoke and anaesthetic bombs."

"If we can find a way out," reminded the captain. "We can't go back down those stairs, they've probably got projectors all lined and ready to blast as soon as we try it." He stared about the small chamber. "There must be some other way, a rear stair, anything. What's behind that door you barricaded?"

"Maybe we'd better find out." Colin reconnected his throat mike and snapped quick orders. "All right, men. Pay attention. We're going to find another way out of this place, we can't try the main gates because the priests are covering the foot of the stairs. Now, here's what we do. As soon as I open this door we make a break for it under cover of smoke bombs. Freeguard, throw down a couple of grenades and when they explode the rest of you follow me. Keep your guns read shoot anything which moves. Ready now."

Jerking his head towards Manson the big man swung the chest away from the door and, as he pulled open the panel, the captain tossed a grenade into the opening. The explosion coincided with those from the foot of the stairs and, before the thundering echoes had died away, smoke billowed from the bombs tossed down to cover their retreat. Wilson gun in hand, Colin led the way through the wrecked door and into the unknown parts of the temple.

Incredibly it seemed deserted. Nothing moved along the twisting corridors and silent chambers furnished in plain but elegant style. Great chests of polished stone stood on the blue-tinted floor and ancient tapestries depicting scenes from the long-dead past hung against the walls. There were no windows, the only light came from the luminescent stone, and the Earthmen trod cautiously through what seemed miles of endless corridor broken by chambers all of which seemed to be the same.

"I don't like this," whispered Manson nervously. "They must know where we are, what are they playing at?"

"I..." Colin halted and turned as a muffled sound came from the rear. "What's that?"

No one answered him. The men stood, their faces pale with tension, their knuckles white from the force with which they gripped their weapons, and stared about the silent corridor. It was Freeguard who was the first to answer.

"Where's Wilner?"

"Wilner?" Colin frowned as he stared at the little group, then, as he automatically counted them, he knew what had happened. Where they had been ten men in the party only eight remained. Somehow, somewhere, two men had been snatched into silent invisibility.

"Stay close," he ordered quietly. "You take the lead, Manson. I'll take the rear. Move!"

Cautiously they trod on their way, each room a heart-stopping peril, every foot of blue-limned corridor a silent menace. Colin walked last, his head half-turned on his shoulder, his ears and perceptions strained for the slightest hint of something wrong.

Deliberately he lagged a little, increasing the distance between him and the nearest member of the party and, as he walked, sweat moistened his features and tension knotted his stomach in anticipation.

Almost he didn't hear the warning.

It was nothing, a stir of air, a sigh, a sense of movement rather than movement itself. Blue luminescence yielded to a black opening and hands, long-fingered and alien, thumbed a weapon which emitted a shaft of yellow vibration. It touched the big man, brushing his shoulder, and he felt the frigid kiss of incipient paralysis, then hands and weapon had dissolved into incandescent flame as the Wilson gun snarled its thunder. Again he fired, again, and smoke and drifting grey ash spilled from the opening. Even as it began to close he flung the tiny bulk of a grenade past the swinging panel of stone, flinging himself flat to avoid the concussion and, as the rolling thunder died away, he tore open the shattered portal.

Priests waited beyond the masked door. Tall and grim in their yellow, mostly dead now, the floor wet with their thin, green ichor, but even as he sprang a yellow robe shifted and a clawed hand pointed the promise of rending death.

A promise, nothing more, for the searing lance of released energy converted the priests, both dead and alive, to scintillant dissolution. Again he fired, again, blasting the room and far doorway with incinerating heat and as the echoes died voices dinned against his ear.

"Colin!"

"I'm all right, Manson. Get the men in here. Quick!"

"No wonder they left us alone," said Manson grimly. "They wanted to avoid damage and thought that they could get us one by one." He wrinkled his nostrils at the acrid smell pervading the room. "Where to now?"

"We follow this corridor." Colin paused, his head tilted as if he were listening. "I think that we must be at the heart of the temple, deep in their private quarters." He kicked a wall. "Metal and thick, too. Luminous like the stone but white light instead of blue. Maybe..." He began to run along the corridor. "Hurry! I've got an idea!"

Desperately they ran after him, slipping a little on spilled green fluid, and as they ran they saw what the big man had in mind. A wounded Martian had passed this way, his blood spotting the metal with slimy green, running from the terrible weapons of the Earthmen and the destruction they had wrought. Colin gasped as he ran, thrusting his long legs against the slick surface and, just as he turned a corner, he saw the priest he was after.

The yellow robe was torn and mired with char and dirt. One arm flapped uselessly at his side and his crest was stained with seeping green. He staggered, half-turned as he heard the thudding feet then, before he could raise a weapon, Colin was all over him.

"Got you!" The big man dragged the helpless native upright. "Now! You're going to show us the way out of this place or I'll burn you inch by inch." He gestured with the Wilson gun in his hand. "Lead us," he commanded, his sibilant gutturals strangely loud in the tense silence. "Lead us or you die!"

It may have been pain, or perhaps a desire to avoid further damage to the precious temple, but it could hardly have been fear for no Martian had ever been known to display fear. Whatever it was, the big man's threat seemed to work for, without a word, the wounded priest led the way. Down a corridor he led them, through a room walled all in metal, another corridor, and halted before a blank door.

"What you seek lies within," he said emotionlessly. "Enter."

"You first!" Colin slammed the native against the metal. "Open it. Quick!"

Silently the priest fumbled at the door, pressing with his one good hand at the blank metal and, without a sound, the door swung open revealing a brilliantly lit interior. For a moment he hesitated then, as Colin stabbed cruelly with the muzzle of the Wilson gun, the native stepped within and the Earthmen follow him.

"The door!" Manson swung shut the thick portal and leaned against it as he wiped sweat from his features. "Colin! Where are we?"

"A laboratory it looks like." The big man glowered at unfamiliar machines, humped equipment and panels of instruments. "I don't get this." He snarled at the Martian. "Is this a trap?"

"This is the way out of your difficulties," said the Martian calmly. "Here is the place you were destined to be, and here you will remain until Dra Vheera comes."

"So it is a trap!" Colin jerked his head as he stared at the instrument cluttered room. "Damn you! I'll wreck the place unless you show me the way out of here!"

"Will you?" Almost it seemed as if the priests would smile, the thin, bloodless lips parted and his one good arm gestured in a slow, indescribably contemptuous motion. "You are a fool, but then, all Earthmen are fools. Destroy this place? I think not. Not unless you wish to destroy others of your own kind, and Terrestrials never do that."

"What do you mean?"

"Listen and learn, dog of an Earthman!" Hate glittered in the slanted green eyes. "Here, within this room, is the vengeance of Dra Vheera. Listen to your fate, scum of Earth!"

Crossing the room the priest threw a switch on an ebon panel, waited a moment, then threw others in quick succession. A low drone filled the room, mounting, then dying as it reached and passed into the upper limits of audibility. Lights flashed on the panel, steadied, then winked like feral green eyes. Deliberately the priest rested his hand on a button.

"Listen. Learn. Tremble before the might of the Dra Vheera. This is your destiny!"

He pressed the button and immediately the room resounded to the scream of a man in extreme agony. An Earthman.

CHAPTER SEVEN

THE VENGEANCE OF DRA VHEERA

It was horrible, that sound. It vibrated from the brightly lit walls like a soul yelling in utter torment and sweat shone on the big man's face as he knocked the Martian's hand from the button.

"Stop it! Stop it, you devil!"

"It offends you?" The priest shrugged. "A sample, no more, of what you can expect by your violation of the temple of Dra Vheera."

"They've got one of our men." Manson clawed at Colin's arm and his face in the brilliant illumination looked sick and ill. "They've got him and are torturing him. Colin! We've got to save him!"

"How?" The big man stared coldly at the captain.

"The priest. He may know of a way."

"There is no way," said the tall native calmly. "But you are wrong. That sound was the recorded reaction of another man when he learned of what his fate would be. A single Earthman who attempted to learn what was not his to know. Your companions, those who suffered beneath the purple flame, they are the lucky ones. They are dead for their sacrilege while you…" He drew in his breath with a hissing sound. "How you will suffer! You dogs who entered our sacred place with weapons in your hands, who have slain the Dra Vheera, who have broken the matrix and ruined the hopes of those who had passed and were to come again. You will live an eternity of pain. You will plead for the death you are so ready to give. You…"

"Shut up!" Colin thrust the priest from him with impatient anger. "You talk too much."

"Dog!" Naked hate glowed in the slanted eyes and, despite his wounds and the pain he must be suffering, the priest made as if to fling himself at the big man. He checked himself as he saw the glowing panel. "So! I talk too much. Then listen to one of your own race, man of blood. Listen and believe!"

Again his hand tripped switches and now, from the concealed speaker, came not a shrieking cry of agony, but a stream of words. Words in colloquial Terran.

"Hello! Hello! Can you hear me? Hello!"

"Who's that?" Colin stepped towards the panel, one arm brushing the priest from his path. "Answer me! Who's speaking?"

"Barnhart. Robert Barnhart."

"What?" Colin glanced at the others then turned again to the panel. "Is this a joke? Who are you?"

"I told you. My name is Robert Barnhart. Terran. Thirty two years of age. Are you Martians?"

"No."

"Thank God for that." Almost the mechanical voice seemed to sob. "I'd almost given up hope that someone won come. It's been so long since I heard a human voice. Where a you?"

"In the temple of Dra Vheera, but…"

"The temple! Are you prisoners?"

"Not yet."

"Good. Then you can help me escape. I…"

"Wait!" Colin dabbed at the sweat running from his forehead. "There's something I don't understand about all this. You say that you are Barnhart's son, and yet I know that you can't be. Whoever you are, wherever you are, that can't be true. Now, who are you?"

"I told you…"

"You told me a lie."

"No! I'm telling the truth. Listen. I tried to investigate the temple, I'm a student of comparative religions, and the priests caught me. They threatened me with something horrible but they must have changed their minds because I seem to be all right. Only it's dark here, and I can't seem to move my arms and legs, and no one speaks to me for a long time. Help me, will you? My father is rich, he will pay you well, but help me."

"I can't."

"Why not?"

"Because," said Colin slowly and deliberately, "Robert Barnhart is dead."

"No!"

"I saw his body, what was left of it." Colin stared grimly at the winking panel. "Well?"

For a long time there was silence, a silence broken only by the hum of strange machinery and the rasping breath of the watching men. Then the voice spoke again, but now it held no hope, no life, only a cold, dead, horror.

"So they did it."

"Did what?"

"They caught me and threatened me with an eternity of punishment. I don't remember what happened then but I remember that I struggled and finally lost consciousness. When I awoke I was in this strange place and the priests were speaking to me. They asked me questions, lots of questions, some of them didn't seem to make any sense at all. Sometimes they spoke of each other as if they had forgotten I could hear and at other times they taunted me with my helplessness. It was horrible." The voice broke then recovered itself. "Where am I?"

"That I don't know—yet." Colin turned and grabbed at the tall figure of the priest. "Listen to me, you spawn of hell. I want the answers to some questions and unless I get them I'm going to watch you fry. What is this thing?" He jerked his head towards the panel.

"A communication device."

"Where is the man speaking?"

"Man?" The native shrugged. "Did you not find his body on the desert?" He staggered as Colin twisted his injured arm.

"I want no riddles," snarled the big man. "Answer or you'll be sorry. Where is he?"

"Nowhere." The priest cringed as Colin lifted the Wilson gun, his finger spinning the focusing device to open wide-aperture. "Wait! You do not understand. His body is dead, yes, but not his mind. That still lives as a crystal as the minds of those who have passed still live as crystals." He shuddered as if he had said too much and Colin turned again to the panel.

"Did you hear that?"

"Yes."

"Did you understand it?"

"I think so. Listen. I was investigating the temple by more means than one and managed to find out quite a lot before they caught me. You know that the natives are all under posthypnotic suggestions?"

"Yes. We saw one of their assemblies."

"Then you know what I mean. Well, you saw the shaft of purple light and the disintegration of the natives. Those men are selected by lottery and they die so that the others can live. Mars is a dying world, you know, and the race increases faster than the fading ecology will allow. War would be one way of solving the problem, but they will not fight between themselves, and so they have reached a compromise. Each year there is a pilgrimage to the temple and those who attend subject themselves to a life or death lottery. Each native registers then sits in a circle and is hypnotised. During hypnosis the globe destroys some of their number, usually about one tenth, by random selection. The unlucky ones are reduced to ash and a crystal but they do not really die. Their electro-potential is locked in the crystal which really isn't a crystal at all but a stress of sub-etheric energy. They are attracted to the green mist and lodge there, their own field currents merging with those of the emerald fog."

"And that fog can be manipulated by varying magnetic currents so as to form a repulsion barrier."

"Yes, you're right, but let me finish, it's important that you hear this. The purple ray reduces the sacrifices to ash and mental stasis but it does more. It releases the life-force and that force is shared between the rest of the assembly. So not only is the race decimated to make room for natural increase, but the entire assembly of worshippers, by absorbing the released life-force, actually extends their own vigour and life expectancy. So there is never any lack of volunteers for the ceremony, they have everything to win and nothing to lose."

"That explains what we saw," agreed Colin. "But it doesn't explain what happened to you. How is it that you have remained aware while all the rest are in stasis?"

"I don't know," said the voice thoughtfully. "The Dra Vheera are subtle and I think that they are using me as a guinea pig. There have been moments…" The whispering drone from the concealed speaker faltered as the trapped intelligence realised its true position. "God! What have they done to me?"

"An eternity of pain," hissed the priest triumphantly. "So end all who violate the temple."

Colin ignored the interruption. What had happened was plain enough. The Dra Vheera knew more of science than the Terrestrials had ever dreamed of. In some way they had divorced the intelligence, the awareness of the ego, from the body and trapped it in a glittering array of sub-etheric energy. Barnhart's son had been so trapped. Now he was nothing but a web of electro-potential connected in some way to the communication device. The most horrible part of it was that the boy obviously couldn't accept the fact that his body had long since been reduced to ashes. He still had hope, still thought he could be helped, and Colin hated to tell him otherwise.

But it had to be done.

"You're dead," he said curtly. "Your body, I mean, ravaged and mutilated and flung on the desert. This thing that is you will never live and breathe again. You are at the mercy of the Dra Vheera and, from what the priest here tells me, he could convert your unnatural awareness to a never-ending hell of agony. You are aware now only because of certain energies which have contacted you. Once this machine is switched off you will plunge into oblivion until such time as they decide to reawaken you. You are an experimental subject, for what I don't know, but they are probably trying to discover what happens to their own people when converted. You will never again experience a normal life."

For a long while there was silence as the frozen intelligence adjusted his viewpoint and accepted what he must have known to be the truth. Then…

"I hate them," the voice whispered. "I despise them. To have all this knowledge and to shield it from us. Like ants they are, a group mind, a tight unity of selfish hate for all things not of Mars. They hate us. Hate us with a terrible scorn and detestation. Beware of the Dra Vheera, whoever you are. Don't trust them."

"I don't." Colin stared questioningly about the brilliantly lit laboratory. "But you may be able to help us. We're trapped here, eight of us, eight Earthmen who tried to discover what the Dra Vheera was all about. Now we must escape. Can you help us?"

"I don't know. There is something I should tell you but memory is vague. A terrible danger, I heard two of the priests talking, something to do with the eventual destruction of Terrestrials and the taking over of Earth by the Martians. A threat. I…" The voice faltered and fell silent.

"A threat?" Colin glared at the sneering face of the priest. "To Earth?"

"Fool!" The tall Martian glared his hate and contempt. "You will learn when you die. By your own hand you will die. Animals. Filth of a fair world. Too long have your kind fouled the deserts of Mars."

"So there is a threat." Colin turned to the panel and appealed to the hidden intelligence locked somewhere within the convoluted coils and mysterious instruments behind the glowing lights. "Bob! Answer me. What is it that we should know?"

"The Elixir." The mechanical voice seemed terribly far away. "Something to do with the Elixir. A thing evolved in the temple laboratories. A delayed action disease, mutated and ready to spring into life after a hundred years."

"Disease!" Colin felt sickness claw at his stomach. "But how? Everyone who can afford it takes the Elixir. It extends the normal life expectancy, restores lost youth, makes an old man young again. How could it be a disease?"

Even as he asked the question he knew the answer. Mutated germs incorporated in the serum, germs which would spread like any other virulent plague but which would not be harmful until they had bred for a certain number of generations. They would lie idle, harmless, lurking in the bloodstreams of the people of Earth until…

Until they bred and changed, and then horror would sweep the Earth as men and women, children and babies, died from the ravages of an alien plague.

And Mars would desert their own, dying world, and settle on the green fields of Earth.

It was cunning, subtle, and typically Martian. They had watched and waited and bided their time. They had read the psychology of men and had found the one weakness which no human could resist. They had traded on the basic desires, the selfishness and greed inherent in the human race, and they had sat back and smiled as man rushed to destroy himself.

For it was so simple. Offer a man restored youth and who would refuse? Offer extended life and millions would fight to be the first to fill their veins with the serum, a serum which, though apparently harmless, contained the seed of a lurking disease. No one would know. No one would guess. They would live and move, contact others and spread the innocuous germs, but all the time, lying in wait for the pre-determined day, those germs would be breeding until their mutated forms changed to something lethal to the human race.

Colin sweated as he thought about it. Thought about the damage already done and the damage which would continue unless…

Unless he could carry the word and the warning, the antidote and the proof.

"Hear me," he snapped. "Listen. You heard them talk and you must have learned a lot. They would be careless before you, for you were trapped and harmless, and even Martians must sometimes like to boast. Did they reveal the antidote? Did they ever say anything to give a clue as to how to kill dormant plague? Think, man! Everything depends on you!"

Silence again, a silence pregnant with the soft hum machinery and, as he waited, Colin was conscious of a peculiar scraping sound. Manson pulled at his arm and gestured with his head.

"The priests," he whispered. "I think that they tampering with the ventilators."

"Watch for gas." Colin turned impatiently towards t glowing panel. "Bob! Hurry! We haven't long."

"A wave-frequency," whispered the voice. "I heard two of the devils mention it and they seemed to regard it as colossal joke. A wave-frequency which could kill the dormant virus."

"Yes? The wave pattern? Quick, Bob, they're breaking in!"

"I don't know the frequency, but it is something peculiar to Earth. I think they said it was the same frequency which men once used for radio-therapy. Wait! I remember now! The secret is engraved on the lid of a small box here in the laboratory. A carved chest, it can't be very big, and the secret is there together with samples of both dormant and active virus."

"Where?" Colin stared helplessly about the instrument-littered room. "How…"

He smiled as he noticed the Martian. The priest had heard every word and, leaning against a humped machine, his slanted eyes had flickered towards a metal cabinet. Three strides took the big man to the cabinet, the butt of the Wilson gun smashed the lock, and he held a small but remarkably heavy box in his arms.

"Got it! Now, can you help us to get out of here?"

"There is an escape tunnel from this room. The Dra Vheera conducted dangerous experiments in here and they built it in case some of their hell-brews should get out of hand. In the corner, I think." The whispering voice seemed to hesitate. "Before you go, there is a favour I would like to ask."

"Yes?" Colin stared across the room to where Manson had lifted a metal flap and was squinting down into a night-filled tunnel.

"I do not want to live like this. Memories are returning and…" The voice faltered. "Must I tell you what I desire?"

"No."

Colin hesitated, the small box beneath his arm, the flare-barrelled Wilson gun pointing towards the glowing panel.

Slowly he levelled the weapon, his finger tightening about the trigger and, just as he was about to fire, Manson yelled a warning.

"Gas! Come on, Colin. Let's get away from here!"

It was true. A thin film of coiling ruby mist seeped from the ventilators and, as a tendril of it brushed across his face, the big man felt his senses quicken. Quickly he threw the metal box towards the captain.

"Take this and get going."

"What are you going to do, Colin?"

"Wreck this place and keep a promise." Jerking a couple of grenades from his belt the big man sprang towards the escape shaft. "Hurry! Get moving, damn you!"

Manson gulped and stepped in darkness, the others followed him, pale-faced, their hands tight about their weapons as they leapt into the unknown. Colin hesitated, staring at the glowing panel and, as he stood there, the wounded priest, almost forgotten in the rush and excitement, flung himself towards the door.

Three strides he took before dissolving into glowing incandescence and Colin poised the grenades in his hand.

"Goodbye, Bob," he said softly. "It's better this way."

"Goodbye, and thanks." The voice hummed from the illuminated panel. "One other thing."

"Yes?"

"Don't tell my father. Let him think I died clean. Let him…"

Gas plumed from the ventilators and Colin swore as he coughed the smoke from his lungs. Deliberately he jerked the pins from the grenades, tossed them to either side of the laboratory, then, the Wilson gun in his hand, turned and jumped into the dark orifice of the tube.

Behind and above him light and thunder converted laboratory, the glowing panel, the trapped and helpless intelligence which had once been a warm-blooded, young man into shattered ruin and semi-molten destruction.

Then he was falling…falling…falling into silence and cloying darkness.

CHAPTER EIGHT

ESCAPE

The tube curved a little as it fell through the building, levelling out like a giant slide so that Colin felt the smooth stone rub against his back as he fell downwards with slowly decreasing speed. As he fell he found time to admire the Dra Vheera for their engineering skill. Of all the ways to escape the possible consequences of a wild experiment such a tube was the best. A man would have fallen several hundred feet during the first few seconds and be well out of harm's way. As he slowed he twisted his body, narrowing his eyes as he tried to peer through the darkness, and holding himself ready for any emergency.

From somewhere in the distance he heard the roar of discharging Wilson guns and the sounds of violent combat and, as the tube levelled still more, he guess that the others had run into trouble.

He was right.

The end of the escape tunnel opened into a small closed room, a vehicle storage for the sand cars lying in neat rows on the smooth floor, and the men who had gone before him crouched behind the switchboard, their guns busy in their hands. Yellow-robed figures darted from doorways, strange energies leaping from alien weapons and, as Colin slid to his feet, a man before him shrieked in the grip of twisting green fire.

He shrieked, staggered, then, as the writhing coils tightened, slumped in tormented death. Again the strange weapon spat its flowing green tendrils, a man dodged, stepped from behind his cover, and stiffened as a ruby beam of lambent heat seared the flesh from his bones.

"Colin!" Manson twisted his head towards the big man. The captain's face was streaked and smeared with the escaping energies of his overstrained pistols and the small metal box lay ignored at his feet. "They were waiting for us. It's a mystery how any of us happen to be alive." He sent a searing lance of energy towards a lurking yellow shape. "It looks as if it is the end."

"Like hell!" Colin narrowed his eyes as he counted his remaining men. Beside himself and the captain only Freeguard and one other man still remained on their feet. Four left out of twenty, and now they had a more urgent reason to escape that that of merely saving their own lives. They held the future of the human race in their hands, the secret of the mysterious plague and the cure for it, and they had to get that box into the hands of the authorities.

Even as he stared at the echoing room the guns were busy in his hands, roaring as they spat their lances of destruction towards alien peril, and the temperature of the air rose the liberated energy scintillated from the blue-limned stone. Priests died beneath that flaming barrier. Their yellow robes fluffing to nothingness, their flesh crisping to ash, their very bones crumpling beneath the lashing fury.

But even as they fell others took their places and the heated air grew thick with the multi-coloured energies from their weapons.

"Manson!" Colin dropped his hand from his empty belt. "Grenades. Where are they?"

"I've got some." The captain swore as his pistol fumed with mounting heat, and flung it away from him as the smooth metal began to turn an ominous red. He ducked as it arched from his hand and exploded with a gush of blue-white flame.

"Freeguard!" Colin yelled above the hissing crackle of electronic weapons, forgetting the microphone at his throat. "Stand by with grenades. When I give the word throw them all over and duck. Immediately after the explosion take that other man and get into a sand car. Understand?"

"Sure, but how are you going to get out of this room?"

"I'll attend to that. Just get in the car and follow me." Colin took the grenades the captain handed him. "Ready?"

"Yes."

"Then throw the grenades."

Carefully, not watching the engineer, the big man lobbed the small package of destruction against the far wall. Sound hammered at him as he flung himself flat behind the shelter of the sand car. Sound and splintered stone, dust and riven bodies, a roaring turmoil of noise and destruction. Before the echoes had died he was on his feet, one big hand yanking the captain up beside him, and together they fell into the cabin of the sand car. Desperately Colin fed power to the engines. The wide treads spun for a moment before gripping the smooth floor then they were lurching forward, directly towards a gaping hole blown in the far wall.

Speed was the one thing which saved them. Speed and the fact that the opening was large enough to permit the cars to pass from the room into the open area of the desert. As the engineer followed the leading vehicle his arm swung up and backwards and fresh explosions sent flat echoes rolling over the ochre plain. Colin grinned with satisfaction as he gripped the guiding levers.

"Do any damage, Freeguard?"

"I don't know." The engineer's voice droned from the speaker against the big man's ear. "Shook them up a little, I think. These cars are tough and concussion doesn't hurt them."

"Lucky for us." Colin swung his vehicle in a wide curve. "Now to get to the rendezvous and away from this damn temple. Stay close behind me and watch for pursuit." He stared at Manson. "Got the box all right?"

"I've got it." The captain nursed his burned hand and kicked at the small metal container. "What happens now, Colin? The Dra Vheera aren't going to let us get away with this and we're three days and sixty miles away from the pick-up point. Once they spread the word we'll have every native on the planet after us."

"That won't matter. I doubt whether they will use energy weapons outside the temple, they don't want the Terran Patrol to know too much about them, so we can hold our own with the Wilson's against their primitive arms." He glanced at a chronometer which he took from an inside pocket. "You're wrong about the time as well. We were longer in that temple than I thought. The rendezvous time is only fifty hours away. In the sand cars we should get there inside three days." He stared thoughtfully at the passing desert. "I'm more worried about the Terran Patrol that I am about the Dra Vheera. The priests are bound to complain and we'll have a patrol on our necks as soon as they can assemble the men."

"Will they though? Complain, I mean?" Manson stared down at the heavy box. "They wouldn't want this to fall into the wrong hands and they know that once we're arrested, we'll tell all we know." He shook his head. "I think you're wrong, Colin. They may complain to the Patrol, but they'll come after us themselves. After all, unless there are Terrans with them, there's nothing to stop them using energy weapons." He slewed in his seat and stared back the way they had come. "I'll bet my share of whatever payment we get that they will be after us as soon as they get organised."

Colin shrugged, not answering, and the sand car slewed and heaved as it rolled over the uneven dunes.

Behind them the tremendous bulk of the temple slowly sank and vanished beneath the horizon. Ten miles passed beneath the spinning treads and still there was no signs of pursuit. Twenty miles and the desert stretched bare and devoid of any living thing to the oddly near horizon. Thirty miles and Colin relaxed as he grinned at the grizzled captain.

"Well?"

"Don't crow too soon." Manson grunted as he checked and reloaded his remaining Wilson gun. "The Dra Vheera never forgive us for what we've done to their temple. That alone would be sufficient to cause our deaths and with what we're carrying they have even a stronger reason for stopping us leaving the planet. I don't like it, Colin. I've got a feeling that they're up to something. We escaped too easily for comfort."

"We were lucky," said the big man easily. "We used force, plenty of it, and they didn't like what we did to them. Those last grenades must have wiped fifty of them out in one go, and they don't want more of the same."

"You believe that?" Manson shrugged. "You know that isn't the answer. The Dra Vheera are fanatics and will die to the last man to stop their secrets falling into the wrong hands. They daren't let us live and you know it."

"I know nothing of the kind." Colin eased up the power as the engines showed signs of overheating. "After all, they may not know what we carry. I wrecked the laboratory when I left and smashed the communication panel. Unless they were eavesdropping they may not even guess that we know all about their plot to murder the human race and take over our planet."

"If you think that, then you're a fool!" Irritation sharpened the captain's words. "Don't underestimate them, Colin. Don't fall into the same error all Earth has been making since we first made contact with the Martians. They aren't primitive. They aren't the simple, proud, easily offended race we think they are. They are a people who are fighting for racial survival and they think less of us than we do of an ant. Damn it, man! Didn't their use of energy weapons tell you that? Their system of decimation, of freezing the released intelligences of those who died selected by the purple ray, of their control of the green mist? Think about it, man. We're like children trying to best adults, ignorance trying to get the better of knowledge—and we're on their own ground."

"Yes," said the big man grimly. "You're right. I'm remembering all that. I'm remembering Barnhart's son, a young man, his body mutilated and thrown out on the desert while his intelligence, the part of him which made him different from all other men, was trapped in a crystal and used as a plaything by the Dra Vheera. I'm thinking of the disease which is spreading through the entire human race, a disease which may spring into virulent life at any moment. And I'm thinking of those men we left behind, all of them!"

Abruptly he turned from the controls and began tearing at his chest.

"Take the controls, Manson." He grunted as he bared compact equipment strapped at his torso. "I hope that this hasn't been injured."

"What is it?"

"Directional radio. I'm going to call the ship and have them come in early. They probably won't be able to make it much before the agreed time but I'll try." He began to operate a key, the pulse signals far simpler and more powerful than the intricate voice wave-pattern normally used. He had barely finished when the concealed speaker hummed behind his ear.

"Colin?"

"Yes?"

"Freeguard here. Can you see anything?"

"What?" Colin lifted himself from his seat and stared back and over the desert. He narrowed his eyes, peering over the rolling dunes but all he could see was the sand and the other sand car.

"I can't see anything," he snapped impatiently. "What is it?"

"You're probably looking in the wrong direction." The engineer sounded almost as if he were amused. "I've been making that mistake too. But look again, Colin. Look ahead and towards the right."

"Wait!" Colin felt sick as he saw what the engineer meant. Ahead of them and a little to the right three plumes of what seemed to be cloud rose in the thin air. But it wasn't cloud, the big man knew that. What he was staring at were the dust plumes thrown up by the treads of three sand cars…now he realised why there had apparently been no pursuit.

The Dra Vheera had swung in a circle, tracking them by some means known only to themselves, and now were cutting them off from the rendezvous point and all chances of safety.

"Shall we dodge them?" Freeguard's voice hummed from the radio as the big man squinted towards the, as yet invisible, vehicles.

"No. We've got to get to the rendezvous, I've radioed the ship to arrive early." Colin chewed at his lip. "If we can see them then they can see us and there are three of them to our two."

"Well?"

"We'll run for it. If we can get to the cairn and set up the Nione we can blow them to hell before they can get near us. Feed your motors power, all you've got, we've got to reach the cairn before they cut us off."

"You haven't a chance." The engineer sounded almost bored. "They're faster than we are and with their lead they can head us off." He paused. "I've got a better idea."

"What?"

"That box is pretty important, isn't it? I heard what was said back in that laboratory and I can guess just what it means to all of us."

"It's important, all right, but what of it?"

"It's not far from the cairn, about five miles I make it. Now, if the two sand cars draw off pursuit a couple of men on foot might be able to make it without too much trouble.

The way things are, with only hand weapons to defend ourselves, we don't stand a chance."

"But damn it, man! What of those who stay with the cars?"

"They still have a chance. If they can dodge the enemy for a while, long enough for you to set up the Nione, say, they can head for the cairn and you could blast the Dra Vheera." Abruptly his voice changed from casual banter to iron resolve. "Don't argue, Colin. You may be the boss but this time it's me who is giving the orders. Stop your car. Derwent will take it over while you and Manson go on by foot. Don't forget to take the box with you and don't get caught. Stop your car now, or better still, keep it moving slowly so that the Dra Vheera won't guess at what we've done."

"No." Colin stared at the approaching plumes of dust. "The plan is a good one but not good enough. You take the box and I'll drive the car."

"Stop arguing." Freeguard sounded too tired to be impatient. "I couldn't walk a mile. I got hurt somehow in the blast, a splinter of rock or something, and I'm oozing blood. Derwent collected a burned leg and a couple of broken ribs. You've no choice, Colin. If you want that box to get through, then you'll have to take it. Better hurry now, those cars are getting awfully close."

He was right, of course, Colin knew that. The box and what it contained was more important than any of them and, if he and the captain were the only fit men left, then they were the ones to carry it. Silently he cut down the power until the sand car was merely crawling along then, without a backward glance, he jumped from the vehicle, the box beneath his arm, and Manson at his heels.

Together, they ran across the shifting sand while, af-ter a moment's pause, the two vehicles suddenly speeded a headed away from them.

Grimly Colin stepped out towards the distant cairn.

CHAPTER NINE

LAST STAND

The journey was a nightmare. For more than two days now they had lived at the peak of tension, fighting, killing, shadowed by the dreadful knowledge of what would happen to them if caught, and their bodies had reached the end of their capacity for punishment.

Around them the desert stretched, alien and hostile, full of secret dangers and hidden perils, of terth, of sand-lice, of grill, an octopus-like creature which first stung, then bled its victims to death. But of all the dangers which threatened them none was so terrible as the vengeance of the Dra Vheera.

They had watched the drifting sand plumes from the speeding vehicles fade into distance, three following two, and Colin wondered whether he would ever see either the engineer or Derwent again. Perhaps if they were lucky they could manage to avoid the net; perhaps, if the Gods were with them, they could circle the hunting cars and make it to the cairn. Colin hoped so, but he doubted it, the odds were too heavy against them.

Tiredly he forced his leaden feet through the clogging sand, Manson stumbling along beside him, both men reeling and staggering at the limits of exhaustion.

"How far?" Manson swayed to a halt, his tongue protruding from between his cracked and swollen lips, words forcing themselves through his constricted throat.

"Not far, a couple of miles, something like that." Colin took a fresh grip on the small box. Almost he hated the grizzled captain for reminding him of his thirst and yet, at the same time, tried to ignore it. Water had been something they hadn't touched for too long. Within the temple they had been too busy to miss it, even within the sand car it hadn't been too bad, but now, exposed as they were to the dehydrating effects of the thin air, their bodies craved for water and thirst was a living flame.

"Two miles!" Manson shook his head. "I can't make it, Colin. I can't just make it." Suddenly, falling as a pugilist would fall, he collapsed onto the ochre sand. "You go on without me. I'm done."

"Don't be a fool!" Colin dragged the other man to his feet. "Walk! The cairn can't be far and we cached our supplies there. Water and food and the Nione gun. Water, man! Water!" Deliberately he swung his broad palm against the other man's cheek. "Damn you! Do you think Freeguard and Derwent sacrificed themselves just so you could sit down? Do you think the others died so that you could give up now? Walk! Walk or I'll burn your feet to ash!"

"Sorry." Manson rubbed his smarting cheek and drew a deep breath. "Thanks. I needed that. I'll make it now, Colin. I'll…"

Something boiled from the sand where he had sat. Something rope-like, squat, hard-shelled, a cross between octopus and a spider and the captain screamed as tendrils lashed across his face and drew sudden blood.

"A grill!" Colin swore as he grabbed at the butt of his gun. "Hold still!"

The thunder of the weapon sent flat echoes rolling over the desert as the brilliant shaft of flame seared the horrible creature to greasy ash. Manson staggered, one hand touching his torn and blood-stained cheek, hardly aware of what had happened. Colin grabbed his arm and began to run across the desert.

"Hurry. If there are any Dra Vheera around they will have heard the sound of that shot and come to investigate." Desperately he forced the stumbling man over the rolling dunes. "Look! That must be the cairn, that piles of stones on the edge of the horizon. See?"

Manson nodded, then, as he turned, stiffened with sudden fear.

"Dust plumes? Ours or…"

"We can't take chances." Colin stared about him, at the barren desert, at the endless dunes utterly devoid of any form of cover. They had to hide, but how?

"Down!" He forced the captain onto the sand. "Bury yourself. Quick! Dig in and cover yourself with sand. It's our only chance."

"But the sand-lice?"

"Let them eat you. Better a few bites than have the Dra Vheera tear you apart." Sand flew as the big man burrowed his way into the side of a dune. "Cover your head with your robe and lie still. No matter what happens, lie still!"

Tensely he waited in the darkness, his head engulfed with his dun-coloured robe, the sand over his body and skull feeling like a premature grave.

At first it wasn't so bad. His overstrained body welcomed the rest and respite from continued effort but then, as the sand-lice discovered the succulent meat and precious water in their domain, life turned into a living hell. A thousand jaws met in the tender parts of his body as a thousand tiny insects seized on his flesh. Pain forced him to bite his lips until the blood ran down his chin. Pain almost caused him to leap to his feet and rip the tormenting insects from his flesh. Almost, but not quite.

Vibration warned him, the transmitted hum of engines and the sand-shaking throb of spinning treads. The vibration stopped and, dimly through the covering robe, he could hear the sibilant gutturals of Martian.

"Anything?"

"No. Perhaps a trap, these Earth dogs are clever at setting traps, and a timed pistol could have caused the sound."

"Perhaps, but…" A pause and then fresh words as if the speaker had seen something of great importance. "See? A dust cloud and not of our making. There!"

"After them!"

Metal clanged and engines whined as the sand car slewed and spun away, the throb of its treads growing fainter as it headed for the distant dust cloud.

Colin gritted his teeth as he heard it go, forcing himself to wait, to resist the impulse to spring to his feet away from the biting torment. Finally, when he judged the vehicle had passed the horizon, he rolled from his cover and cautiously regained his feet.

The desert was clear. Hastily he found Manson, lifting the captain to his feet and stripping the clusters of red crab-like insects from his flesh. Then, when they had rid themselves of their tormentors, they resumed their journey towards the distant cairn.

Two hours later they stumbled among the heaped stone, almost too weak to find and recover the cached supplies, then as soon as they had drank some of the precious water, they set up the long barrelled Nione gun and settled down to wait.

"You think they made it?" Manson stretched himself where he lay among the stones and squinted over the darkening desert. Colin grunted from where he stared over the barrel of the gun.

"No idea. Perhaps, perhaps not. Nothing we can do now, anyway."

"When will the rocket arrive?"

"Soon. I radioed to it a short while ago and they're heading in now. The trouble is the time was set for two days from now and they can't make it all up."

"I hope they get here in time." Manson stared up at darkening sky. Stars shone against the deep depths of space, cold and remote, somehow mocking as they stared down at the petty doings of men. A faint wind blew from the horizon, chill with the promise of night, and Manson shivered as he kept his vigil, watching for the men who might never come.

"Better get some rest," ordered the big man quietly. "I'll stand first watch."

He squatted behind the smooth metal of the long-range weapon as the captain, worn out with his exertions, slept through the frigid night. Dawn came with a wash of pink and gold, waking the older man with its warming light, and he took Colin's place, resting his hand on the firing levers as he stared at the featureless desert.

At mid-day he woke the big man.

"What is it?" Colin rubbed his blood-shot eyes and peered to where the captain pointed.

"Something's moving out there." Excitement made Manson's voice even more high pitched than normal. "See?"

"Yes." Colin thinned his lips as he saw the tiny shapes. Dark they were against the horizon, small, distant and yet unmistakable.

The hordes of the Dra Vheera.

"They must have caught the sand cars," whispered Manson dully. "Now they know that we are here. How would they know that?"

"Can't you guess?" Colin didn't trouble to hide his bitterness. "If they caught the sand cars they may have caught either Freeguard or Derwent alive. Or perhaps they caught them and realised that there were two men unaccounted for. Perhaps they can trace the box by some built-in radiation. I don't know."

"What would have happened had they caught one of them alive?"

"Curious, aren't you?" Tension made the big man snarl at the captain. "What do you think would have happened? You've been bitten by sand-lice. How would you like to be stripped and staked out on the dunes? Smeared with bait perhaps? Your own blood would do for that and it wouldn't take long for the sand-lice to really get to work. How long could you remain silent? Especially if you were wounded and delirious, weak with thirst and mad with pain." Anger made the big man grip the controls of the Nione. "Damn the swine! Damn them! Damn them!"

"If only the rocket would come." Manson stared up at the bright bowl of the heavens. "To have come so far, to have done so much, and now…" Sweat shone on his face as he stared at the advancing specks. "What will they do to us, Colin?"

"Kill us—if we make them. Torture us if we let them." The big man stared contemptuously at the older man.

"What are you worrying about? We knew what could happen when we started all this. Get a grip on yourself, man. You can't aim straight if you're afraid of being hurt." He frowned at the nearing shapes of the Dra Vheera. "Listen. If one of us gets killed then the other must do his best to get the box to Earth. Hide it with your body if you have to, but make sure it gets on the rocket."

"Yes." Manson seemed to have lost his fear. "I know what you mean."

"Good. Now we've still a little time. They don't know that we have a Nione and will be a little too confident. Have something to eat now and drink all you can. Load and check your weapons. Get everything ready for a long, hard fight. Make some shelters among the rocks so that we can shift our line of fire. Get busy now!"

Colin grinned as the captain busied himself about his tasks. His own weapons had long since been checked loaded, he had made shelters, and knew that that all they could do had been done. But with something to do the captain lost his fear in work and the big man knew the value of a steady brain when it came to the final combat.

He ate a little, scooping the vitamin paste from a can and washing it down with a little water. Then, slowly and calmly, he settled down to wait for the attack.

It came almost before he expected it. It came with a rush of yellow-robed priests and the scintillant flash of alien weapons. The air burned to the searing heat of electronic discharges and stone glowed red and ran in molten ruin beneath the touch of green coils and ruby beams, splintered to the touch of sapphire stars and shrilled with resonance as yellow rays crystallised the age-old stone.

Then the Nione opened fire.

Thunder rolled to the near horizon and light, brighter than the flaring sun, limned the desert with incandescent brilliance. Energy flamed from the tapered muzzle, a cleansing, destroying flood of searing brilliance, roaring with the full fury of exploding atoms and shocking the snarl of the alien weapons to stuttering silence. Where the flash of destruction had touched was nothing. No priests, no advancing shapes, no creeping figures. Like a hose of fire sprayed on a column of ants so the power of the Nione had washed away all opposition.

But not for long.

Again the terrible weapon spouted its ravening charge of energy, again, again, but now the Dra Vheera had learned from experience and less and less of them fell to the cleansing flame.

And two men, no matter how well armed, cannot hold out forever against a thousand fanatics armed with weapons almost as good.

Slowly the yellow-robed priests crept nearer, hiding behind the shielding dunes, advancing from all sides, rushing forward when the Nione fired opposite to where they lurked, and hiding again when the long barrel swung their way. And they returned the fire.

Heat singed the hair from the big man's head and energy tore the flesh on the side of his head. One arm went numb as a sapphire star expanded its soundless violence against a rock, and blood stained the dun-coloured robe a richer hue.

Manson screamed as he felt his ribs snap and sear his lungs, swore as the smell of his own roasting flesh irritated his nostrils, and gulped as he stared at the blistered stump where his left hand should have been.

"Steady!" Colin spat a mouthful of blood and triggered the Nione. "Keep firing, Manson. Keep firing!"

"For how long?" The captain cursed with frightened weakness as he aimed and fired, aimed and fired, squeezing the trigger with mechanical desperation. "Where's that damned rocket? Where is it?"

"I…" Colin swore and flung himself away from the long barrelled weapon. Green fire writhed around it, merging with the dull red glowing at its base, and the big man knew only too well what was to come. He grabbed at Manson, flung himself down over the stones, and cowered, hands against his ears as he waited for the explosion.

It came, a shaking, man-made thunder, and, when the smoke and singeing rocks had fallen and died, he became of a frenzied shooting.

"The rocket! The rocket! Colin! The rocket!"

It was true. The slender shape dropped on its pillar of flame and, as he saw it, the big man sprang to his feet and searched desperately for the box.

"Come on. Quick, before the Dra Vheera recover from the explosion!"

Impatiently he ran across the shifting sand towards beckoning silver shape. Behind him ran Manson, staggering, spitting blood, weaving and stumbling as he tried to maintain the pace. Behind him ran the Dra Vheera.

Colin reached the rocket just as the port opened and without a backward look, he flung himself into the interior. Manson shrieked as he ran, a wordless plea for help, a cry to those in the steel shell to wait for him and take him to safety then, as a yellow-robed priest aimed a weapon, screamed beneath the searing agony of green fire.

"Take-off." Colin thrust at the outer door. A ship officer stared at him and made as if to pull if open.

"Blast you!" Anger leant the big man strength. "He's dead. They're all dead, all of them except me, and I'll be dead if you don't take-off. Move!"

He collapsed then, sagging down to the cool metal but, even as he hit the deck, he felt the pulse of the engines, the savage venting of energy as the flaring rockets lifted the ship up, away from Mars, back to the cool green hills of Earth.

www.ingramcontent.com/pod-product-compliance
Lightning Source LLC
Chambersburg PA
CBHW020659180626
46816CB00003B/1356